Fire and ice

Camilla caught her breath as his thumb invaded the neckline of her shirt to brush against her leaping pulse, that beat in the hollow at the base of her throat, and her tongue parted her lips when his gaze dropped to her mouth.

"I'm sorry," Alex said huskily, and for a minute she hadn't the faintest idea what he was talking about.

"Are you?" she got out breathily, and, unconsciously, she leaned toward him. His mouth was only inches from hers, and she ached to feel it moving against hers....

"Yes," he replied, but now the husky note had hardened to a harsh denial, and as he stepped back his hand fell away. "I guess we all make mistakes," he added and, brushing past her, he took the stairs two at a time.

ANNE MATHER began her career by writing the kind of book she likes to read—romance. Married, with two children, this northern England author has become a favorite with readers of romance fiction the world over—her books have been translated into many languages and are read in countless countries. Since her first novel was published in 1970, Anne Mather has written more than eighty romances, with over ninety million copies sold!

Books by Anne Mather

STORMSPELL
WILD CONCERTO
HIDDEN IN THE FLAME
THE LONGEST PLEASURE

HARLEQUIN PRESENTS

1251—A FEVER IN THE BLOOD
1315—A RELATIVE BETRAYAL
1354—INDISCRETION
1444—BLIND PASSION
1458—SUCH SWEET POISON
1492—BETRAYED

HARLEQUIN ROMANCE

1631—MASQUERADE
1656—AUTUMN OF THE WITCH

ANNE MATHER

Diamond Fire

Harlequin Books

TORONTO • NEW YORK • LONDON
AMSTERDAM • PARIS • SYDNEY • HAMBURG
STOCKHOLM • ATHENS • TOKYO • MILAN
MADRID • WARSAW • BUDAPEST • AUCKLAND

Harlequin Presents first edition December 1992
ISBN 0-373-11514-8

Original hardcover edition published in 1991
by Mills & Boon Limited

DIAMOND FIRE

CHAPTER ONE

ALEX doubted he would have noticed her if she hadn't been having an argument with the clerk at the car rentals desk. She had apparently travelled from Los Angeles on the same flight he had, but he hadn't noticed her on the plane. Which wasn't too surprising. The United Airlines 747 had been full, and unless she had been sitting right next to him the chances of his recognising a stranger among so many passengers was slight.

Besides, he had spent most of the five-hour journey studying Morales's report. It was inconclusive, he knew, but he had hoped it might offer some clue the other man had missed. It didn't. The trail the investigator had followed to the mainland dried up in San Diego, and, although Alex was pretty sure Virginia was heading for the Mexican border, without a definite lead it was futile for him to pursue it.

In consequence, he had left it in Morales's hands and flown back to Honolulu. There was always the chance that there might be some message at the house; some means through which he might be able to contact her. And that was how he came to be standing in the arrivals lounge, waiting for his own lift, idly watching the woman crossing swords with the Chinese girl at the car rentals agency.

It was her hair that held his interest. He had never seen hair quite that colour before. It was red, a rich vibrant red that seemed to throb with a life of its own. And, although it was presently coiled in an increasingly precarious knot on top of her head, he could imagine how it would look if it were loose.

Not that he was interested, Alex thought ruefully, hardly able to remember when he had last felt any real sexual stimulation. In recent years, Virginia's frantic demands for sex had destroyed any desire he had felt to

5

make love with her, and even when he found out what was wrong with her the feelings he had once had for her were gone.

Lately he had begun to wonder if the girl he had thought he had married had ever existed outside his own imagination. He suspected that, as far as Virginia was concerned, marrying him had just been a means to an end. She had needed a home; money; security; and he had had it all. Quid pro quo.

Of course, it hadn't been enough; he realised that now. What Virginia had been seeking didn't exist either, though her methods of dealing with it had left him cold. Perhaps it was his fault, as she had claimed. After six years of marriage perhaps he should have felt more responsibility. But there were limits to his sympathy; limits to his credibility; limits to his patience. Virginia didn't want to change; she would never change. And he was not the gullible idiot he had been when she had married him. Five years of trying to stop someone from destroying herself had seen to that.

Even so, when he'd left for New York a week ago he had not realised how near the edge she was. If he had, he told himself now, he would never have gone. But he had a business to run; he had commitments. And babysitting Virginia could be a full-time job.

Nevertheless, the night before he'd left she had seemed almost normal. They had actually held a conversation during dinner, and he certainly hadn't suspected what she was planning. If they had had a row he might have been on his guard, but they hadn't. It had all been perfectly amicable. Which should have been a warning; but it hadn't.

He caught his breath as fear gripped his stomach. He had never dreamt she might leave the island. In spite of everything, she liked the comfort of their home, the sybaritic delight of wearing fine clothes, of sleeping between silk sheets. If nothing else, Virginia appreciated luxury, and there'd be precious little of that where she was going.

But it wasn't fear for his wife that caused the knife to turn inside him. She might be desperate, but Virginia could look out for herself. It was their five-year-old daughter, whom Virginia had taken with her, who was causing Alex so much pain. The daughter Virginia had never wanted, until she could use her against him.

'*Signore*, I am here.'

Carlo Ventura's quiet voice distracted him, and Alex turned to the man, who had worked for the Conti family since before Alex himself was born, with enforced civility.

'Carlo,' he said, inclining his head, noticing as he did so that the red-haired woman had apparently abandoned her efforts to make any headway with the car rentals agency, and was presently striding out of the building. She had nice legs, too, reflected Alex unguardedly, and then, impatient that he could think of such things at a time like this, he let Carlo take his briefcase, and fell into step beside him. 'Has there been any news?'

'No, *signore*.' Carlo shook his greying head regretfully. He was several inches shorter than his employer, and he had to look up to meet Alex's dark eyes. 'No word at all, *signore*. I am sorry.'

Alex's silence was eloquent of his feelings. They emerged into the moist air of the afternoon with a shared sense of frustration. There was only so much he could do, thought Alex, sloughing the jacket of his silver-grey suit and draping it over his shoulder. With the best will in the world, he could only guess at Virginia's destination. And in a city the size of San Diego it was all too easy to disappear. A woman and a child travelling alone were not conspicuous. He supposed he ought to be grateful that she was on her own. If some other man had been involved, what price his daughter's safety then? All he could do was leave it in Morales's hands, until he found a lead that was hopeful.

The dark blue Mercedes that Carlo had driven to the airport to meet him was waiting just outside. Although it was being eyed rather contentiously by the traffic policeman sitting astride his motor cycle by the taxi-stand, it hadn't as yet received a ticket, and Alex was relieved. He raised his hand in greeting as he recognised the uniformed patrolman who had granted the dispensation, and as he did so he saw the redhead again, this time climbing into the back of one of the cabs that plied for hire between the airport and Waikiki. He guessed she was one of the many holiday-makers the islands attracted throughout the year. There was no real 'season' in Hawaii, and tourists arrived at all times of the year. Most started their holiday in Oahu, and Waikiki was still the most popular resort in the whole of the Pacific.

He noticed she wasn't wearing a *lei* around her neck, and he wondered if she had visited the islands before. He, too, had sidestepped the proffered garland, but in his case it was familiarity, rather than any desire to offend the smiling *wahine*. Most people found the custom of being greeted with a necklace of orchids rather charming. But evidently her arrival had not been all it should be.

And then, irritated with himself again for allowing his attention to be diverted, Alex tossed his jacket on to the back seat of the Mercedes and slid behind the wheel. He wished he had only the frustration of not being able to find a hire-car on his mind. How nice it would be, he thought, to put everything but his own personal needs out of his mind.

Carlo was busy supervising the porter, who had accompanied them outside, opening the trunk and having the man stow Alex's suitcase inside. Then he walked round to join his employer. 'OK, *signore*,' he said, slipping into the seat beside him. And Alex put the car into gear, and relaxed as the powerful engine carried them away from the airport.

It was good to be in control of his transportation again, even if he was not in control of his destiny, Alex thought wryly. He had always believed he was in control of both, but recent events had taught him that nothing in life was sure.

He drove into the city first. As Carlo had said there was no news at the house, he wanted to call at his office on the off chance that there might be a message there. From Morales perhaps, he reflected hopefully. It was more than twenty-four hours since he had spoken to the investigator, and he had told him to keep him informed of any development, no matter how small.

The route into the city took him along Nimitz Highway, past the familiar sight of the Dole Pineapple Cannery, and into downtown Honololu. The syrupy scent of the cannery that assailed his nostrils as he drove over the Kapalama Canal bridge was vaguely reassuring, but for once the sight of the pineapple-shaped water tank failed to give him a lift. Even the marina, where his own yacht, the *Maroso*, was moored, warranted only a passing glance, the nodding heads of the sailing craft like flamingos against the blue horizon.

Although the skies out at the airport had been dull and overcast, Honolulu and nearby Waikiki were bathed in unbroken sunshine. Which was the reason the island was so popular, Alex knew. It seldom, if ever, rained on Waikiki Beach, and the soft showers that did fall melted in temperatures that soared into the eighties. Indeed, it was another of the island's boasts that the gentle breezes that played along its shoreline never allowed the heat to become oppressive. It was hot and often humid, but never unbearable.

The Conti building stood in Ala Wai Boulevard, not far from the First Hawaiian Bank. It was one of the many skyscrapers that had begun to dot the Honolulu skyline in recent years, and it mingled congenially with the smaller though more architecturally impressive buildings around it. Visitors were always intrigued by the way old buildings jostled cheek-by-jowl with modern constructions, with parks, churches and palm trees offering peaceful oases of shade.

Carlo waited in the car while Alex went up to his office. The Conti Corporation, which had been founded by his grandfather between the wars, had now expanded its operations into most of the major industries of the world, and the building was a hive of activity. As managing director, Alex was its senior executive, with a highly skilled team of consultants working with him. His father, retired now but still active, had retained the title of chief executive officer, but it was a nominal position at best. To all intents and purposes, Alex was in charge, and he had the final word in any controversy.

However, since Virginia had disappeared, Alex had spent little time in the office, and he had been glad to leave any decision-making to someone else. With interests that ranged from import and export to logging, from coal-mines in Europe to steel-mills in Asia, from oil in

Canada to emeralds in Columbia, the company would
have been impossible to operate successfully without his
delegating responsibility. It was one of the things his
father had taught him, after his grandfather had died
of a stroke at the age of forty-nine, and he had been
glad of that knowledge during the past week. Apart from
anything else, he wouldn't have trusted his own
judgement in his present state of distraction, and it wasn't
fair to make mistakes when so many people's livelihoods
were involved.

'Mr Conti!'

Sophy Ling, one of a pair of secretaries who occupied
the outer office, greeted him with genuine warmth, and
Alex forced a smile in response. 'Hi, Sophy,' he said,
nodding at her and her companion. 'Have there been
any messages for me?'

Sophy looked as regretful as she felt, and Alex guessed
that the news of Virginia's disappearance had percolated
throughout the whole building by this time. He had
hoped to avoid the inevitable publicity it would create,
and as yet he was not being accosted by reporters wanting
to know what was going on. But it would come, he knew
it. Which was another reason for keeping away from the
Conti building.

'Is Grant in his office?' he asked now, avoiding any
overt expressions of sympathy, and Sophy's companion,
Rose Fraser, said that he was. Grant Blaisdell was his
cousin and his personal assistant, and in Alex's absence
he had been running the operation. 'OK. I'll be in Mr
Blaisdell's office, if you need me.'

'Mr Conti . . .'

Evidently Sophy hadn't got the message, and Alex had
to steel his features as he turned to speak to her. 'Yes?'

'We—that is, Rose and I—we were sorry to hear about
Mrs Conti,' Sophy ventured tentatively. 'If—if there's
anything we can do . . .'

'There's not.' Alex managed to keep his tone pleasant
with an effort. 'But thanks anyway. It's appreciated.'

Grant's office adjoined the executive suite, a room
only marginally smaller than Alex's own office. Like his,
it had a magnificent view over the whole of Honolulu,

with the familiar sight of the Aloha Tower marking the waterfront.

Grant himself rose from behind a square mahogany desk as Alex came into the room. The son of Alex's father's sister, Grant owed his appearance more to his father's New England ancestry than to his mother's Italian forebears, and in consequence, although he was as tall as Alex, he was much lighter skinned. But since Grant had joined the company five years ago the two men had worked well together, and Alex knew his aunt was relieved that her son had finally found his niche in the Conti empire. Until then he had been employed in a variety of occupations, most of which Alex would have put under the heading of free-loading. Grant hadn't wanted to work, and for six years after college he had wandered all around western Europe and the mainland, only coming home when he'd needed funds.

But five years ago he had had a change of heart, and Alex had not been averse to taking him on as his assistant. He was family, after all, and it just so happened that his former assistant had left at around the same time, creating an opening. Of course, Alex knew that several senior members of the board had had reservations about the appointment, but so far Grant hadn't let him down. On the contrary, he seemed keen to learn everything he could about the corporation, and, as Alex was fond of his aunt, he was glad his reports were always favourable.

'Alex,' Grant said now, shaking his cousin's hand and gesturing towards the couch set beneath the almost floor-to-ceiling windows. 'Is there any news?'

Alex grimaced, and eschewed the offer of a seat. 'I was about to ask you that,' he said, shoving his hands into the pockets of his trousers. 'I left Morales in San Diego yesterday. I haven't heard from him since.'

'San Diego?' Grant's blue eyes widened. 'Is that where Virginia is?'

'I doubt it.' Alex was laconic. He felt weary, and he didn't honestly feel up to a long discussion. 'My guess is she's heading for Mexico. It's the only thing that makes any sense.'

'Ah.' Grant nodded, aware of what his cousin was thinking. 'So...can I get you a drink?'

'No, thanks.' Alex shook his head. 'I just called in to tell you I'm back, and that I'll come into the office tomorrow morning. Right now I'm going to go home and try to get some rest. I feel as though I could sleep for a week.'

'So, why don't you?' exclaimed Grant swiftly. 'There's nothing spoiling here, and I can handle anything that comes up. With Rose and Sophy on my case I wouldn't be allowed to make any mistakes. And you do look tired, Alex. I mean it. Take a break.'

Alex took his hands out of his pockets and walked to the door. 'I'll see you tomorrow,' he said, ignoring Grant's snort of resignation. He managed to grin. 'There are only five years between us, *cugino*. I'm not ready for retirement yet.'

'OK.' Grant raised his hands defensively, palms outwards. 'I guess I should know better than to try to persuade you. But, just in case you do have a change of heart, I'll be here if you need me.'

'Thanks.'

Alex's inclination of the head was grateful, but faintly ironic. He had the feeling that, barring a miracle, he would make it into the office the following day. Without Maria the house was so empty, and he couldn't bear the silent sympathy in the faces of his servants. Besides, he hated the inactivity, the sense of helplessness he felt at not knowing where his daughter was, where Virginia had taken her. At least at work he could find some escape from the fears he had for her safety.

His own office offered no more reassurance. His desk, cleared of all but his personal correspondence, looked bare and unnaturally tidy. The reports and papers that usually cluttered its leather surface had been passed to someone else to deal with, and the room seemed to emphasise the emptiness he felt. Damn it, he thought, if he could lay his hands on Virginia now he'd be tempted to wring her neck.

The phone rang as he was standing by his desk, his clenched fists balled against the wood. The sound was doubly startling in the quiet room, and he pounced on the receiver, his stomach muscles clenching. Could this possibly be Virginia? Had his rage against her somehow brought her to the phone?

It was his father, and Alex sank down into the soft leather chair that abutted his desk as Vittorio Conti's harsh tones rang in his ears.

'*Alex? E tu?*'

'*Si, Papa.*'

Alex answered in the tongue his father always used on the telephone. It was Vittorio Conti's belief that one never knew who might be listening in to one's call, and in a country where English was the common language there were obviously fewer people who understood Italian. That was why he insisted that his son be as fluent in that language as he was in his own, and why Alex didn't hesitate before responding in the same way.

Now Vittorio continued, 'I tried the house first, but Mama Lu said you still hadn't arrived from the airport. I guessed you must have called in to speak to Grant. Is there still no news of their whereabouts?'

'No.' Alex was abrupt, but he couldn't help it. The bitter disappointment he had felt upon first hearing his father's voice and not Virginia's still gripped him, and it was with the utmost effort that he relayed a résumé of Morales's report to Vittorio.

'San Diego, eh?' His father repeated the name with a comparable note of frustration in his voice. 'What in hell does she think she's doing? She must know that sooner or later we'll catch up with her.'

'I don't think Virginia does think. At least, not with her brain,' said Alex wearily. 'She just acts; on instinct, mostly. She wants something, and she goes after it. She doesn't care who she hurts in the process.'

'But to take Maria——'

'Look, Papa, I'd really rather not prolong this discussion, if you don't mind. I'm bone-tired, and I'd really like to get home. I'll phone you and Mom later, if there's any news. OK?'

'OK.' The old man seemed to sense that his son was nearing the end of his tether, and he backed off. 'I'll expect to hear from you later, then.'

'Yes, later,' said Alex gratefully. '*Ciao*, Papa. And—
thanks for calling.'

Outside again, Alex breathed in deeply the cooling air
of late afternoon. As the sun sank in the sky, the city
streets became cool canyons of shade, and, in spite of
his internal turmoil, Alex couldn't prevent the sense of
relief he felt to be back on the island. Increasingly hectic
though Honolulu was becoming, it was his home, and
he loved it.

Carlo didn't do him the injustice of bothering to ask
if he had learned anything new. He knew that if Alex
had heard anything he would have told him, and he remained silent as his employer drove north along
Kapahulu Avenue. The roads around the capital were
busy with a mixture of tourists and home-going com-
muters, but, once beyond the city's limits, Alex could
relax. The powerful Mercedes would have eaten up the
miles, but he kept it within the speed-limit. He was in
no real hurry to reach home, whatever he had told his
father.

He took the main highway across the southern flank
of the island, and then drove north again along the coast
road. The scenery here was spectacular, but although
Alex saw the long golden stretches of sand, with the pale
aquamarine water creaming on the shoreline, he was in
no mood to appreciate them. He was remembering his
daughter's fear of her mother's moods, and that without
Mama Lu to intercede on her behalf she was vulnerable.

The Conti estate lay just beyond the Waiahole Valley,
where orchids and anthurium blossoms grew in such
profusion. It was a farming area, with fruit orchards
and quiet meadows grazed by handsome horses, defying
the hand of the developer. But Alex's home was on the
seaward side of the road, and the curving track that led
from Kamehameha Highway resisted any efforts to in-
filtrate his privacy. Besides, at the gates to the estate he
employed a very efficient security staff to ensure that no
unwelcome visitor got in. The pity of it was, he thought
now, that they had had no jurisdiction to prevent anyone
from getting out.

A lush jungle of palms and wild hibiscus formed a
natural barrier between the private road that led to the

estate, and the manicured lawns beyond. Alex noticed that the white flowers had come into bloom in his absence; combined with the more familiar red blossoms of the hibiscus the effect was startling. Like blood on white linen, he reflected fancifully, and then dragged his thoughts from the precipice where they were heading. Virginia wasn't going to defeat him, he told himself grimly. But the knife turned just the same.

Kumaru, his house—the house that had once belonged to his father, but which Alex's parents had moved out of when Vittorio had retired—stood on a rise, with the ocean at its back. It had been Alex's home for as long as he could remember; firstly as a much-loved only child, and then later, after his marriage to Virginia, they had occupied the self-contained wing that his father had had built on to the main building. Alex suspected that his mother and father had not originally intended to move out of their home. But circumstances had changed their minds. Although they had never criticised Virginia in his presence, it had become increasingly obvious that the two households could not exist side by side. Virginia had made no secret of her dislike of his parents, and, although they loved their only grandchild, when Vittorio had given up his active role in the corporation they had moved into a smaller house, nearer the city.

The house itself was a long, sprawling, ranch-style dwelling, with most of the rooms on the ground floor. But, as the house was built on sloping land, a lower-ground floor gave space for what had used to be his mother's garden room, a sauna and gymnasium where Alex expunged much of his frustration, and a play-room for Maria. Mama Lu's quarters were there, too, next to the play-room. The old Hawaiian woman, who had been first his nurse and was now Maria's, also acted as unpaid housekeeper, for Virginia had never been interested in looking after her family. It was all 'too boring': her words, not his. Besides, why should she bother about such things, when that 'stupid old woman' was perfectly willing to do it?

Things had changed a lot since the days when his mother had taken a pride in supervising the running of her home, Alex thought now, bringing the car to a halt on the pebbled forecourt. Although she had been a *haole,* or a newcomer to the island, having been brought up in New England and coming to the island for the first time when she married Vittorio, Sonya Conti came of good middle-European stock. In consequence, she had never been prepared to leave her household in the hands of servants. She had been there, ever vigilant, caring for her home and her family, creating the comfortable ambience her husband had needed after a day at the office.

Not so Virginia. Alex had invariably been greeted by some complaint about himself, or Maria, or one of the servants, and her ever-present craving for excitement had soured the whole atmosphere of the house. Indeed, were it not for the fact that she had taken with her the one person Alex loved more than anyone else in the world, he might have welcomed her disappearance. Though, he conceded wearily, knowing what he did about her mental condition, he doubted he could have abandoned his responsibilities completely. Family ties were too strong, and his upbringing had been such that he would not, in all conscience, have left her to her fate.

Now he thrust open his door to get out, but before he could pull his jacket from the back seat a small bald-headed man came rushing out of the house. Dressed in baggy black trousers and a dark green mandarin jacket, his olive-skinned face alight with animation, he came crunching across the pebbled drive towards the car. It was Wong Lee, Alex's steward and Mama Lu's husband, and Alex felt his stomach tighten at the probable cause for his excitement.

'*Padrone!*' he exclaimed, skidding to a halt beside the car. '*Padrone*, you have a visitor.'

Alex endeavoured to control his quickening heartbeat. 'A visitor?' he echoed, as Carlo, too, got out of the automobile. 'What kind of a visitor?'

'What kind of a visitor?' Wong Lee's eyes registered his confusion. 'What kind of visitor were you expecting?'

'The *padrone* was not expecting a visitor,' snapped Carlo shortly, his superiority of service giving the edge of impatience to his voice. 'What the *padrone* means is—is his visitor on business, or pleasure?'

'Thank you, Carlo, I can handle this,' Alex inserted swiftly, sensing the potential for conflict and in no mood to encourage it. The fact that Mama Lu was still apt to spread her favours rather freely sometimes created other problems, and, although both Carlo and Wong Lee were in their sixties, sexual rivalry knew no age limit. 'Who is the visitor, Lee?' His palms felt damp. 'Is it someone from the mainland?'

'Yes, sir,' replied Wong Lee, giving Carlo Ventura a triumphant look. 'She says she's Mrs Ginia's cousin. She says Mrs Ginia invited her to come visit.'

Alex's brows descended. 'Virginia's cousin?' he echoed disbelievingly, and then, before either Wong Lee or Carlo could make any further comment, he tossed his jacket over one shoulder and strode towards the house. Virginia's cousin, he brooded as he mounted the two shallow steps that led up to the veranda. He couldn't remember Virginia ever mentioning any *female* cousin, and he was pretty sure he hadn't met her at the wedding. The marriage, which had taken place in London, had been a fairly large affair, it was true, and it was possible that there had been cousins of Virginia's there that he had never been introduced to. But, as far as he knew, Virginia's mother had been an only child—much the same as Virginia, he reflected now, with similar characteristics—and her father had supposedly died in the dim and distant past. Indeed, so far as Virginia's relatives had been concerned, they had been rather thin on the ground, and the majority of the guests had been friends and acquaintances, and his own rather large circle of relations.

So, who was this woman? he wondered grimly, tossing his jacket on to a polished Japanese chest in the hall, and raising questioning eyebrows at Mama Lu, who had heard the car and was making her own, less energetic way to greet him. At something approaching two hundred and fifty pounds in weight, the elderly Polynesian woman was not disposed to hurry anywhere, and Alex had sometimes wondered at her apparent irresistibility to both Carlo and her husband. In Alex's estimation, she could have crushed either of them between her massive thighs, but evidently he was not privy to her undoubted sexual attractions.

Now, however, he was not in the mood to consider such anomalies, and when she opened her mouth to say, 'There's a lady waiting to see you,' Alex cut her off unceremoniously.

'I know,' he said, breathing deeply. 'Who is she, and where is she?'

'Well . . . she says she's your wife's cousin,' murmured Mama Lu, glancing towards the louvred doors that led into the parlour. 'I put her in there.'

'Thanks.'

Although Alex knew that the old woman would have liked to accompany him into the parlour, his tone was dismissing, and Mama Lu knew it. But as she turned away Alex saw her reddened eyes, and, realising she was as upset over what had happened as he was, he made a rueful gesture.

'I'll let you know why she's here as soon as I find out,' he promised, and Mama Lu's fat cheeks wobbled a little as she summoned up a tearful smile.

'Shall I make some tea?' she suggested, and, although tea was the last thing Alex needed, he nodded.

'Yes,' he said, guessing she needed something to do. 'That's a good idea.'

Mama Lu inclined her head, and ambled away towards the kitchen as Alex took hold of the handles of the doors. Then, forcing away the uneasy feeling of impending disaster, he slid the doors aside.

The young woman who was waiting for him was standing by the windows. Which meant she had probably observed his arrival, he thought grimly, giving her plenty of time to prepare for this meeting while he was still on edge at learning of her presence in his house. Was that why she appeared so calm and composed now, when only hours before she had been the one who had lost her temper? he wondered warily. For it was the woman from the airport, Alex saw instantly. The redhead who had been having the argument with the girl at the car rentals desk. The woman who had attracted his unwilling attention long before he had known who she was—or who she *claimed* to be.

CHAPTER TWO

ALEX was nothing like her expectations. From Virginia's description, Camilla had imagined a man in late middle-age, with a balding pate, and a paunch. A man who was mean and cruel, more concerned with making money and running his business empire than with taking care of his young wife. He had married her because he'd needed a wife to provide him with an heir, Virginia had written, and after making her pregnant he had eschewed his responsibilities. Consequently, she was left alone and neglected on this isolated country estate, desperate for company, desperate for a friend.

And, of course, all that could be true, she conceded now, steeling herself to meet his dark-eyed gaze without flinching. Just because he was younger than she had expected, and infinitely better looking, was no reason to doubt that his character was every bit as black as Virginia had painted it. The trouble was, it seemed that Virginia wasn't here, and now Camilla felt like the protagonist and not the defender.

'You're...Virginia's cousin?' he enquired politely, and Camilla, who had told the lie in order to get beyond the gates of the estate, felt a faint trace of colour invade her pale cheeks.

'Not—not exactly,' she admitted, wishing Virginia had not chosen today of all days to absent herself from the estate.

'Not exactly?' Alessandro Conti's dark brows ascended towards the dark swathe of hair that dipped on to his forehead. 'Either you are, or you aren't. Don't you know?'

'My name is Camilla Richards——'

'Really?'

'Yes, really.' His drawl, which had echoes of the west coast of America in its depth and resonance, was at-

19

tractive, but she refused to be diverted. 'Um . . . Virginia . . . and I went to school together. We've known one another for . . . for over fifteen years.'

Alessandro Conti's expression didn't alter. It was still cold, and watchful, and infinitely suspicious. It made Camilla feel as if she had done something unforgivable by coming here, and she began to believe that Virginia had not been exaggerating.

'So—you're not my wife's *cousin*,' he said at last, and Camilla reluctantly shook her head. 'Then do you mind telling me what the *hell* you are doing here?'

Camilla swallowed. 'Well, really——'

'Well, really—what? Did Virginia send you here, is that it? Did she tell you to get in here by whatever means you could? What does she want? Are you her messenger? Because if so I should tell you, *Miss* Richards——'

'No!' Camilla broke into his angry tirade with a denial that fairly trembled off her tongue. 'No, of course Virginia didn't *send* me here! I don't know what you're talking about. Virginia *invited* me to come. I'm her guest. And . . . and when your . . . your bloodhound at the gate refused to allow me to come in I said I was Virginia's cousin, because it seemed the only thing to do!'

Alessandro Conti's eyes narrowed. 'D'you want to run that by me again? You say—Virginia *invited* you here?'

'Of course.' Camilla held up her head proudly, becoming aware, as she did so, that the knot she had secured so confidently in the hotel in Los Angeles that morning, was rapidly loosening, and fiery strands were beginning to tumble about her nape. 'We . . . we went to school together, as I said, and when she wrote and told me——'

'Told you what?'

'That . . . that . . .' Camilla faltered. She could hardly tell him *exactly* what Virginia had said, but at the same time she had to give some reason for her precipitous arrival from London. 'She—er—she said why didn't I take a holiday in Hawaii? That . . . that it would be fun to . . . to talk over old times. I . . . I naturally thought you knew about it.'

'Me?'

Alessandro Conti pointed towards his chest, and Camilla couldn't help noticing the shadow of hair and skin beneath the fine material of his shirt. The shirt was made of silk, she thought, and it encased a broad chest and muscled biceps, the cuffs rolled back to reveal hair-covered wrists. Like the dark trousers that covered his legs, and moulded the undeniable evidence of his sex, it had obviously been made by an expert hand, and in one aspect at least, she guessed, Virginia had not been mistaken: her husband was obviously a wealthy man.

'Me?' he said again now, shaking his head. 'You thought Virginia would have discussed it with me?'

Camilla licked her dry lips. 'Yes.'

'Then you obviously don't know your...*friend*...very well,' he declared harshly. 'Exactly when was this invitation issued? And what do you propose to do now?'

Camilla frowned. 'I beg your pardon?'

'I said——'

'I know what you said.' Nervousness had made her defensive. 'Are...are you implying that I can't stay here?'

The look he gave her was incomprehensible. 'You expect to stay? Now? In the present circumstances?'

Camilla gave a helpless little shrug. 'What circumstances?'

'The fact that Virginia's not here,' declared Alessandro Conti impatiently. 'I understood someone had told you that.'

'Well—yes.' Camilla was confused. 'But ... she'll be back, won't she?'

'Will she?' He took a couple of steps nearer to her, and all at once she was aware of her own vulnerability in the face of this tall, daunting stranger. 'You tell me. *When* will she be back?'

Camilla swallowed. 'Well—I don't know exactly, of course. La ... later today, I suppose.'

'Later today?' He was barely an arm's length from her now, and, although she kept telling herself that he had no reason to suspect her of any wrong-doing, his attitude was so strange that she inwardly retreated.

'I ... don't you expect her back at any time?' she stammered, resisting the impulse to raise her hands in front of her. For God's sake, what had she said? He was acting as if she herself were responsible for Virginia's absence.

There was a pregnant silence while she fought the urge to put some space between them, and he studied her face with those dark, disturbing eyes. And then, almost dismissively, he told her, 'Considering that Virginia disappeared almost a week ago, I should say it was highly unlikely that I'd expect her back today, wouldn't you?'

The room she had been shown to was unlike any room Camilla had occupied before. As a fairly successful solicitor, working in Lincoln's Inn in London, she had used her fairly generous salary to travel all over Europe, and on one occasion she and a friend had even ventured as far as Sri Lanka for a holiday. But no hotel room had ever compared with the luxury of this apartment in Alessandro Conti's house, and, although she didn't want to be, she *was* impressed.

And why not? she thought ruefully, after the incredibly fat Polynesian woman, who had originally admitted her to the house, had left her alone. She might consider herself moderately sophisticated, but she wasn't used to split-level rooms, with velvet carpets on the upper level and polished floors strewn with expensive Chinese rugs on the lower. She wasn't used to beds the size of a small football field, or ceilings with curved fanlights, angled so that there was no danger of being dazzled by the sun.

Not that the sun was a problem right now, she had to admit. On the contrary, darkness had fallen with an unexpected swiftness, and, although she was sure that the view from the veranda outside the room would be equally spectacular as what she had found within, the velvety blackness outside her windows was almost opaque. But she could hear the ocean murmuring somewhere beyond the terrace, and in spite of the unexpectedness of all that had happened she couldn't prevent a prickling sense of excitement.

After all, she was here, on Oahu, just a few miles from the world-famous Waikiki Beach which Rupert Brooke had described so evocatively all those years ago. She had never been so far from home before, and, although

Virginia's disappearance was worrying, Camilla wouldn't
have been human if she hadn't felt some stirring sense
of communion with her surroundings. Hawaii was one
of those places that everyone dreamed of visiting at some
time in their lives, and from what she had seen of it so
far it lived up to every one of her expectations.

Which was more than could be said for her host, she
admitted unwillingly. Alessandro Conti had proved to
be the exact antithesis of the impression Virginia had
created in her letter, and it wasn't easy to ally what
Virginia had written with the man she had met. Oh, she
knew appearances meant little. In her work she had had
to learn to distinguish between a clever lie and an un-
clever truth, and sometimes the most unlikely story
proved that life was often stranger than fiction. And she
had no reason to disbelieve the things Virginia had told
her. Nothing Alessandro Conti had said had given her
any real reason to doubt his culpability. On the contrary, she was quite prepared to believe he could be violent on occasion, and there had been a moment during
their conversation when she had felt threatened. Yet, for
all that, she was uneasy with the situation, and it wasn't
just because Virginia wasn't here.

But where was she? she wondered, turning to view her
two suitcases, placed side by side on a long cushioned
ottoman at the foot of the enormous bed. She was here,
as Virginia had requested—no, *begged*—but Virginia,
and her small daughter, had apparently run away.

It didn't make sense. Why would Virginia invite her
here and then disappear? Why would she imply that she
was virtually kept a prisoner, and then leave the island
without telling anyone where she was going? And why
take Maria with her? The little girl's father was obviously worried sick about his daughter. That much she
had gathered. As to his feelings about Virginia's disappearance, they were less easy to interpret. She thought
he was worried about his wife, but there was something
else, something he wasn't saying, but which his words
were telling her. Perhaps Virginia was right. Perhaps he
did regret marrying her. Perhaps if she had attended the
wedding she would not be so perplexed now.

But she had been in Italy when Virginia had married Alessandro Conti, and in any case after they'd left the private girls' school they had both attended their lives had diverged. For one thing, Camilla had only attended the expensive boarding-school because her godmother had paid for her to do so when her own parents were killed. Mr and Mrs Richards had died in a climbing accident in Switzerland when Camilla was ten, and, although for a while her godmother had found it amusing to play nursemaid to her orphaned god-daughter, eventually the inconvenience of having to make arrangements for baby-sitters every time she had wanted to go out had begun to pall. In consequence, at the age of thirteen Camilla had been despatched to Queen Catherine's, and she had remained there for the next five years.

Virginia's circumstances at that time had not been unlike her own, and she supposed that was why the two of them had become such friends. Virginia's mother— her father was never talked about—was one of those brittle women who spent their lives relying on other people to support them. Camilla supposed Virginia's mother had had some money once, but that had long since been squandered on expensive clothes and other luxuries that outwardly showed she could hold her own among the social élite with whom she claimed parity. Virginia's school fees, like Camilla's own, had been paid by some long-suffering older relative, but by the time Virginia left school her mother was in real financial difficulties.

In consequence, Virginia had been expected to recoup the family fortunes by marrying well, and, although Camilla would have hated such a responsibility, Virginia had seemed perfectly resigned to her fate.

That it hadn't happened as swiftly as her mother could have hoped had been made apparent when Camilla met her friend for lunch, about a year after leaving Queen Catherine's. By this time Camilla had been anticipating her second year at university, and although it was a struggle financially she was determined to get her degree. Although she'd still occasionally seen her godmother, and would be eternally grateful to her for being there

when she'd needed her, she'd had no intention of
sponging on her again. With her grant, and the ad-
ditional cash she earned by working at a fast-food restaurant in the evenings, she had been keeping her head
above water—just—and, if her life hadn't exactly been
glamorous, at least it was satisfying.

Virginia, meanwhile, had changed from the rather free
and easy teenager she had been at school. Camilla hadn't
wanted to believe it, but already her friend was beginning to speak like her mother, and there was a
sharpness to her personality that had not been there
before. In addition to which the differences in their life-
styles had created a gulf between them, and, while
Camilla was interested in what her friend had been doing,
Virginia had a totally different set of values.

Of course, Camilla had made excuses for her. She
knew it couldn't be easy living the kind of brittle existence that her friend's mother found so appealing.
Virginia wasn't like that, not really; at least, Camilla
had never thought so. And if she did seem self-centred
now, it was probably just a front. It was Virginia's way
of handling a difficult situation.

It was another two years before they had met again,
and then only by chance in Bond Street. By this time,
Camilla had achieved her hard-won degree in law, and
was having an equally hard struggle in finding some firm
of solicitors willing to give her a chance to get her
articles. Until she had spent at least two years working
as an articled clerk in a solicitor's office she could not
begin to call herself a lawyer, and, in those days of high
inflation and unemployment, it wasn't easy.

Virginia, however, had been jubilant. She'd insisted
they went into a nearby wine-bar that she knew, and
over champagne cocktails, which Camilla had paid for,
she told her friend that she was getting married. A certain
wealthy Argentinian polo-player was her constant escort,
and both she and her mother were planning a Christmas
wedding.

Camilla had been suitably enthusiastic, although the
prospect of her friend's marrying some South American
playboy just because he was incredibly wealthy had filled
her with unease. Virginia might appear to be on top of

the world, but there was a distinct edge to her brilliance,
and Camilla hadn't been able to help noticing she seldom
looked her in the eye for more than a few seconds. And
she was so thin, almost unfashionably so, if that were
possible. And talking of a glittering future about which
she hadn't seemed convinced.

Of course, there was nothing Camilla could have said
to dissuade her, and nor did she try. She was rapidly
coming to the conclusion that the Virginia she had known
at Queen Catherine's might not have been the real
Virginia at all, and although she blamed the girl's mother
it wasn't really all her fault.

However, Virginia's Christmas wedding had not materialised. A month later the wealthy Argentinian polo-
player had eloped with an American model, and although
Camilla was not involved she'd felt tremendous sympathy. She guessed how humiliated Virginia must have
felt, and wished there was something she could do.

But there wasn't. She knew no one who might re-
motely meet Virginia's demands so far as a husband was
concerned, and the idea that her friend might realise the
futility of the life she was leading, and find some other
way to assuage her needs, was no longer even a
possibility.

And then, nine months later, out of the blue, Camilla
had received an invitation to Virginia's wedding. Not to
the Argentinian playboy, of course. He had long since
married his American model, and was presently in the
process of adapting to fatherhood. No, Virginia's
husband-to-be was an American businessman,
Alessandro Conti, and after the wedding they were to
live at his luxurious estate in Hawaii.

It had sounded like a dream come true, Camilla had
to admit, except that she herself knew nothing about
this American businessman. He was not someone whose
face had appeared in the British tabloid press, and
Camilla had assumed that was because he was not considered sufficiently newsworthy to warrant the kind of
gossip status accorded more photogenically viable per-
sonalities. She supposed that was where she had first got
the idea that Alessandro Conti must be some kind of

Howard Hughes figure: wealthy perhaps, but too old to enjoy camera notoriety.

The fact that she now knew how wrong she had been didn't alter the fact that Virginia had married this man, probably without knowing very much about him beyond the fact that he could keep her—and her mother—in the manner to which they had both become accustomed.

However, her chance to see Virginia's proposed husband for herself had not materialised either. The precipitate arrival of Virginia's wedding invitation had coincided with her own annual holiday, and by the time she had returned to London the wedding was over, and Virginia departed for pastures new. An interview with her mother, brought about by the fact that Camilla had not known where to send the handmade lace tablecloth she had brought back from Italy as a wedding present, had elicited an address in Oahu, but apart from a hurried note of thanks they had shared no further communication. For six years!

And then, just like the invitation to her wedding, Virginia's letter had arrived without warning, sent on to Camilla's present employer by one of the clerks in the office where she'd used to work. Evidently, Virginia had listened to some of what Camilla had told her, and although she had not remembered her address she had remembered where she worked.

Which was just as well, Camilla thought now. She had moved twice since those early days at Farquahar and Cummings, and there was every possibility that a letter sent to her previous address would have gone astray. Or perhaps it would have been better if it had, she reflected with some cynicism. At least then she would not have had to read Virginia's impassioned prose, or flown out to Hawaii at the drop of a hat with the distinct impression that she was on a mission of mercy.

For Virginia had said some pretty damning things about this husband of hers in her letter. For one thing, she had implied that he was mistreating her, and Camilla had been half afraid she would come here to find her friend covered in bruises. The marriage had been a mistake, Virginia had stated passionately, the words she had used bringing her thin, agitated face to mind. Alex—

she had called her husband Alex—didn't care about her;
she doubted he ever had, and she was going mad with
no one to talk to. Could Camilla come to Oahu? She
knew it was an imposition, but she had no one else. Her
mother had apparently been taken ill some time ago,
and was presently being cared for in a nursing-home in
Surrey, and Virginia couldn't burden her with her
troubles. Please come, she had pleaded. For old times'
sake. She would be forever grateful.

But now Camilla was here, and Virginia wasn't. For
some reason—some final humiliation, perhaps—she had
abandoned all hope of deliverance and run away, taking
her daughter—Alessandro Conti's daughter—with her.
Camilla thought it was probably just as well she had
taken the child with her. Otherwise, given what Virginia
had told her about him, she might well have suspected
her husband of being involved in her disappearance.
After all, Alessandro Conti, by his own admission, had
known nothing of the letter Virginia had sent to England,
and so far as he was concerned there was no one who
might question her absence. The servants were obviously devoted to their master, probably because he paid
them well to be so, Camilla decided uncharitably. They
wouldn't raise a finger to help their mistress. Indeed,
there seemed a distinct lack of concern for Virginia's
safety from everyone, including her husband. They
wanted her—and the child—back again. But not, apparently, because of any great affection for her.

Camilla shook her head. It was hopelessly confusing,
and she was finding it increasingly difficult to hold at
bay the headache that had been plaguing her ever since
Mama Lu, if that really was her name, had admitted her
to the house. She wanted nothing so much as to lie down
on the enormous bed and give way to the after-effects
of prolonged jet lag, but instead she was supposed to
wash and brush up, and join her host for supper. After
convincing himself that Camilla really had no more idea
of Virginia's whereabouts than he had, Alessandro Conti
had summoned the Polynesian woman again, and had
had her show their guest to this apartment. Apparently
he had decided that she should be offered their hospi-

tality for tonight at least, and Camilla had been left alone, to unpack her suitcases and take a shower.

Shaking her head a little bewilderedly now, Camilla picked up her handbag and rummaged about in the bottom for the strip of aspirin tablets she kept there for emergencies such as this. Breaking the foil, she popped two tablets in her mouth, and then looked about her for something to swallow them with. There was no obvious container for the purpose, and, realising she could get water from the tap, she walked into the adjoining bathroom Mama Lu had indicated.

She stopped short then, momentarily stunned by its luxurious appointments. As well as a smoked-glass shower cabinet, there was an enormous sunken bath with whirlpool jets, and twin hand-basins of lime-green porcelain that matched the other fitments. Once again, there was a bulging skylight overhead, but right now the room was illuminated by long strips of light concealed above the smoked-glass mirrors that lined the walls.

It was all a bit too much for her to cope with at the moment, and, collecting a smoked-glass tumbler from beside the array of bathroom accessories and cosmetics that were arranged in a hand-woven basket between the basins, she filled it from the tap and swallowed a mouthful of water along with the aspirin tablets. Then, setting the tumbler down again, she stood for a moment studying her reflection in the mirror above the basin.

She looked tired, she thought critically, but that wasn't really surprising. Yesterday she had flown from London to Los Angeles, a journey of some ten hours, and this morning she had caught a delayed flight to Honolulu, which had added another five and a half hours to her travel time. That, combined with a ten-hour time change, made staying awake at any hour of the evening a distinct effort. After all—she glanced at her watch—her body-clock was still working, at least partially, on British time, and right now it was about five o'clock in the morning in London.

The Polynesian housekeeper had told her that Mr Conti usually ate his evening meal at around nine o'clock, which gave her plenty of time to take a shower—

or a bath, if she chose—and rest for a while before having to face him again.

Which was just as well, she reflected, pulling the remaining pins out of her hair. The expensive perm she had had before leaving England had not tamed her hair, as she had hoped, and now it tumbled about her shoulders, an uncontrollable mass of crinkles. Of course, the sea air on the journey from the airport hadn't helped. After reading about the sophistication of American cars she had expected the taxi to have air-conditioning, but if it had the driver had found no use for it. He had driven along with the windows wide open and the invading breeze had been as destructive as it had been welcome. What Alessandro Conti must have thought of her, she couldn't imagine. Even her suit was crumpled, and, together with the lines of fatigue around her rather pale eyes, she looked altogether unprepossessing.

She was simply not one of those women who looked good in any circumstances, she decided, turning away from the mirror. Her features were acceptable, it was true, but she needed make-up or she looked washed out. Another consequence of having such violently coloured hair, she thought impatiently. Still, in her own world, and her own time, she managed quite successfully, and there had been one or two men over the years who had seemed to find the combination of a mobile mouth and a bubbling sense of humour sufficient compensation. Not men like Alessandro Conti, she had to admit. But then, men like Alessandro Conti didn't look for their women among career-minded individuals who didn't regard sex as the be-all and end-all of existence, Camilla reminded herself defensively.

Half an hour later she emerged from the bathroom wearing the towelling bathrobe she had found on the back of the door, and feeling a little better. With reckless abandon she had taken both a bath and a shower, using the latter to wash her hair and cleanse her body of the expensive gel that had created a storm of bubbles in the jacuzzi. It was only afterwards she had realised that she probably shouldn't have used the bubble-bath in conjunction with the jets, but by then it was too late. Besides, she thought defiantly, Alessandro Conti could

afford to have it repaired if she had caused some damage.
Clearly, a shortage of material assets was not the reason
Virginia had decided to leave home. If hers was just an
example of a guest-room at the house Camilla could imagine what the master suite must be like.

Padding, barefoot, across the velvet carpet, she
switched on the television set that resided on a bureau
opposite the bed, and then padded back to sit on the
satin coverlet. She had at least half an hour to fill before
she needed to start getting ready, and watching television would take her mind from the chaotic jumble of
her thoughts. Time enough later to consider what she
was going to do, she decided, settling herself back against
the pillows. For the time being she was not going to
worry. In spite of her claims to the contrary, Virginia
had proved she was not a prisoner, and until Camilla
heard differently she would have to assume she could
take care of herself.

CHAPTER THREE

CAMILLA awoke to unfamiliar sounds—the call of doves from the nearby trees, the shrill cry of a sea-bird, the muted roar of the ocean. For a moment she couldn't remember where she was, or how she came to be here, and she came up on her elbows, blinking as she looked about her.

And then recollection returned to her—or a selective part of it did anyway. She was in Hawaii; on the island of Oahu; and in Alessandro Conti's house, Kumaru, to be precise. She had arrived there the previous afternoon, only to find Virginia wasn't here; but she had been shown in to this room, to relax and refresh herself before supper.

She frowned then. For that was as far as her recollection took her. She clearly remembered being shown into this room, and she also remembered taking a bath and washing her hair.

She put up a wary hand to her hair, but apart from a faint slickness, which could have been caused by sweating as she slept, it felt quite dry. But—and it was at this point that a wave of embarrassment swept over her—she was naked beneath the sheet, which was all that covered her. And that simply wasn't usual. She never slept in the nude. Indeed, she invariably wore old, baggy cotton T-shirts to sleep in, but for this trip she had bought herself two rather glamorous nightgowns from Janet Reger. She had not known if Virginia might still want to indulge in bedtime confidences, and, guessing the kind of nightwear she would favour, Camilla had invested in something she need not feel ashamed of. That was why she felt so uneasy now. She was sure that on this occasion particularly she would not have put herself to bed without her nightgown.

Which meant...

A flush stained her cheeks. The conclusion was obvious. She must have fallen asleep watching the television, and someone else—Mama Lu, probably—had decided not to disturb her. Instead, the bathrobe had been whisked away, she had been covered with the sheet, and her hair left to dry on the pillow.

So what?

Refusing to allow herself to continue down this avenue of thought, Camilla threw back the sheet and slid her legs over the side of the bed. Her nakedness disturbed her, but a swift rummage in one of the suitcases still residing at the foot of the bed produced the satin dressing-gown that matched one of the nightdresses. Wrapping the robe about her, she immediately felt more in control of her destiny, but the memories still rankled.

God, she thought, pushing back the weight of her hair with a frustrated hand, as if the situation hadn't been complicated enough, without her behaving like some first-time traveller. For heaven's sake, it was bad enough that she had arrived here unexpected and unannounced, without falling asleep at a time when she was supposed to be having supper with Virginia's husband!

She sighed. Well, he didn't have a particularly flattering opinion of her anyway, she consoled herself. It was obvious he had originally believed that Virginia had sent her here to intercede on her behalf, and when she had finally convinced him that this wasn't so he had still regarded her with some suspicion. *With some suspicion!* Camilla shook her head disbelievingly. As if he had any reason to be suspicious of *her*! She was a solicitor, for God's sake. She was paid to deal with other people's transgressions, not to be accused of transgressions of her own.

Still, he had seemed to accept her story—or at least an edited version of it—by the time the housekeeper was summoned to show her to this room. Indeed, he had been unexpectedly courteous once he had satisfied himself that she was not actually lying to him. She hadn't been given the impression that he totally trusted her story, but he certainly hadn't rejected it.

But now she had undone all the good work she had achieved the night before. Alessandro Conti was hardly

likely to remain convinced of her professed concern for
Virginia's whereabouts if she could drop off to sleep as
if she hadn't a care in the world. He might even see it
as proof of her complicity, and her heart sank at the
probable outcome. If he insisted that she left here now
she might never find out what had happened to Virginia,
and, for all her helpless loss of consciousness, she was
worried.

However, there was nothing she could do about it.
Virginia's husband would decide what course her stay in
Oahu was going to take, and for the present she could
only prepare herself for the worst.

But the sun was shining, filtering in through the printed
silk curtains that someone had drawn over her windows,
and Camilla would not have been human if she hadn't
felt a sense of curiosity about her surroundings. Stepping
down on to the lower level, she crossed the delicately
patterned rug, and drew the drapes aside.

She startled a brightly coloured bird that had been
breakfasting from the tumbling branches of an azalea,
whose rose and lilac-coloured blossoms spilled over the
balcony; but Camilla scarcely noticed. Her widening eyes
were drawn to the brilliant waters of the Pacific surging
on to a stretch of almost pure white sand just a short
distance away. From a creamy whiteness, caused by the
reflection of the sand through the water, to the deepest
blue on the horizon, the water shaded from lime to jade,
from robin's-egg pale to sapphire, an ever-changing
carpet of shifting colours.

Camilla caught her breath. She had never seen such
a delightful sight before, and for a moment she forgot
everything in the sheer pleasure of just looking. It was
so unbelievably beautiful, and the isolated prison of
Virginia's letter seemed far from this enchanted place.

Fumbling with the catch that secured the sliding glass
doors, she eventually discovered how to open them, and
stepped out on to the iron-railed terrace. The air was
surprisingly cool, but only cool by Hawaiian standards,
she reflected dreamily. Even at this hour of the morning,
the inherent warmth, which would invade the atmosphere later in the day, was already a sensuous promise
against her legs. The playful breeze had parted the skirt

of her robe, and was exposing her long slim legs to the strengthening rays of the sun, and because she was alone with the morning she let it do its worst.

What time was it? she wondered. She had removed her watch before her bath, and now, reluctantly, she turned back into the room and climbed the steps again to the sleeping-deck. She found her watch on the table beside the bed, and discovered it was only half-past six. Evidently, the time-change had worked to her advantage this morning. The household wasn't yet stirring, but she was wide awake.

She discovered, when she went to take her shower, that fresh towels had been placed on the rack in the bathroom, and new phials of bath gel and shampoo had replaced the ones she had used the night before. She shook her head in wonder. It was like staying at the very swishest hotel, she thought, remembering an article she had read about a chain of hotels in New York that actually employed somebody to anticipate the guests' every whim. She had the feeling that if she had arrived without her suitcases that would have been taken care of as well! Alessandro Conti probably left nothing to chance.

But then, she reflected as she dropped her robe on to the laundry basket and stepped into the shower, she was obviously not the usual sort of guest he entertained. She could imagine politicians coming here with their wives; congressmen, or senators, perhaps; people well known in the arts and education; scientists; maybe even a judge. And also, perhaps, some people who operated outside the law. Alessandro Conti was clearly of Italian descent. He might even belong to the Mafia.

Deciding she was allowing her imagination to run away with her, Camilla abandoned this train of thought and concentrated on what she was doing. The shower was strong and invigorating, pummelling her scalp and the tender skin of her breasts, flowing in rivulets down the lower contours of her body. Watching the water disappear through the grill at the bottom of the shower, she was reminded of the scene in the film *Psycho*, when the erstwhile heroine of the piece was invaded by the deranged owner of the motel. She remembered the shadow through the curtain, the knife blade raised and then falling with such horrible intent——

'*Aloha!* Miss Richards!'

Camilla nearly jumped out of her skin. The shadowy bulk beyond the shower screen was much too close to what she had been thinking, and she dropped the shampoo, and had to scrabble about in the bottom of the shower to find it again.

Then, realising it was only the housekeeper, she straightened. 'Y... yes?' she called, annoyed to find her voice betraying the shock she had had. 'Wh... what do you want?'

'I have left a tray of coffee in the bedroom,' Mama Lu replied imperviously, and Camilla could see her reflection through the glass, moving round the bathroom, picking up her robe and folding it over her arm. 'I guessed you might wake early this morning. If you would like me to bring breakfast to your room I will, or you might wish to take it outdoors.'

Camilla swallowed her resentment that the housekeeper should come into her room without knocking, and cleared her throat. 'Um... I think I'd like to have breakfast outdoors,' she said, wondering if Alessandro Conti would like to join her. 'Er—thank you for the coffee. I'm sure I'll enjoy it.'

'You're welcome.'

The housekeeper drifted out again, and, expelling a trembling breath, Camilla completed her toilet. She had washed her hair again, deciding it would be easier to style damp than dry, and after drying her body she put on the fresh towelling bathrobe Mama Lu had left in place of her own.

It would have been easy to feel some impatience with the housekeeper for taking her own robe away, but she supposed Mama Lu was only being helpful. Camilla simply wasn't used to having servants lay out her clothes for her, or provide her with her own pot of coffee that tasted just as delicious as it smelt.

Abandoning any hope of remaining businesslike in these surroundings, Camilla dressed in cream cotton Bermuda shorts and a collarless silk blouse. The elbow-sleeved blouse was patterned in shades of cream and green, and was cool without looking too holidayish. The last thing she wanted Alessandro Conti to think was that she was regarding the present situation as a holiday. She might have told him she had come here with that intent, but obviously now that was not the way it was. On the contrary, in the clear light of day Virginia's disappearance was no less disturbing. Camilla couldn't understand why she should have done it. She must have expected her friend to respond to her summons, and, as soon as she had received Virginia's letter, Camilla had made arrangements to do so. She hadn't sent a cable, for obvious reasons. But there had been no reason for Virginia to lose hope so quickly.

Perhaps she hadn't run away. As Camilla plaited her hair down the back of her head and finished with a short braid that nudged her shoulder she wondered if it was at all possible that Virginia had simply decided to take a trip without telling anyone. It was irresponsible, of course, but when they had been at school together Virginia had been irresponsible sometimes. Looking back, Camilla had to admit that her friend hadn't always done what was expected of her. So why shouldn't she have arranged this trip and taken her daughter with her?

Deciding it was at least something she could suggest to Alessandro Conti, Camilla finished her coffee, took one last, rather resigned glance at her reflection, and left the bedroom.

The hall outside was bathed in sunshine. Long windows that overlooked the lawns at the side of the house had not yet had their blinds slatted, and the floor was striped in bands of gold. As in the lower half of her room, the floor itself was made of wood, polished around the heavy fringed rugs that were laid at intervals along the corridor. Camilla looked to left and right, and then started in what she hoped was the direction of the wide arching vestibule she had entered the night before.

The house was huge, but she had known that before she had started out. Arriving yesterday afternoon, she had had some intimation of its size from the windows of the taxi that had brought her from the airport, but inside it was even more daunting. Halls and passages led off in all directions, and, while initially she had the side of the house to guide her, when she turned a corner even that reference was denied her.

The corridor ahead of her now ended in a pair of double-panelled doors, and, although she gazed at them with some expectation, Camilla was almost sure she hadn't come this way the night before. She was lost, and she decided to make her way back to her own room and start again.

But as she turned away she heard the sound of a door behind her opening, and when she cast a hopeful glance over her shoulder she saw Alessandro Conti striding towards her. Immediately her heart sank. For heaven's sake, she thought irritably, he would probably think she was searching the house, and she briefly closed her eyes against a fate that decreed she should meet this man again in difficult circumstances.

However, there was nothing she could do about it now. He had seen her, and, watching him come towards her, Camilla was again struck by his disturbing personality. Wearing a pearl-grey suit of some fine material that moulded the powerful lines of his strong body like a glove, he looked every bit as compelling as he had done the night before. And, although she didn't want to notice how the close-fitting trousers accentuated his physicality, she couldn't help it.

'Lost?' he enquired, after wishing her good morning, and Camilla mentally smoothed her ruffled senses and glanced up at him.

'I... Yes,' she answered, obliged to fall into step beside him. 'I'm afraid I must have come the wrong way.'

'It's easily done,' he assured her, his tone not half as brusque as she had expected. 'Did you sleep well?'

'Very well.' Camilla swallowed. 'Which reminds me, I must apologise about last night. Falling asleep like that. I expect Mama Lu told you.'

'Mama Lu?' Alessandro arched an enquiring eyebrow. 'Oh—yes.' He inclined his head. 'You were obviously tired.'

'Even so——' Camilla caught her lower lip between her teeth '—it was unfortunate. I...don't suppose there's any...news?'

'About Virginia?' A perceptible hardness entered his tone as he spoke his wife's name. 'No. No, I'm afraid not.'

Camilla shook her head. 'I don't understand it.'

'No.' The look he gave her was enigmatic. 'No, I don't suppose you do.'

They had reached the main hall, and Camilla looked about her in some surprise. They seemed to have bypassed her room altogether, and were now in the enormous vestibule with its exquisite crystal chandelier suspended above a mosaic-tiled floor. The marble tiles were in direct contrast to the maplewood floor of the corridor and the velvet carpet that had cushioned her feet in the parlour, she thought. Yet they all blended together beautifully, creating an attractive asymmetry of styles. That was one thing Camilla had noticed the night before: the elegant mingling of opposites.

'Have you had breakfast?' her host asked briefly as he led the way through an arched doorway at the back of the hall, and down a half-spiral staircase. The staircase could only lead to the lower level of the house, Camilla realised, following him, and as she did so another figure appeared below them.

'*Padrone!*' he exclaimed politely, spreading his arms in obvious welcome. 'Everything is ready, *signore*.'

'Thanks, Lee.' Alessandro descended the final few steps of the staircase, and turned to wait for Camilla to join him. 'This is Wong Lee,' he added, as she stepped down into what appeared to be a kind of indoor garden. 'He and Mama Lu take care of us—*me*!' The amendment was almost savage. 'Lee, this is Miss Richards. She's from England.'

No mention of the fact that she was his wife's friend, Camilla noticed ruefully as she smiled at the little Chinese man. Well, perhaps that wasn't so surprising in the circumstances, she thought. Virginia's friends were rather thin on the ground around here.

'So pleased to meet you, Miss Richards,' Wong Lee greeted her, bowing from the waist. 'Welcome to Hawaii.'

Camilla smiled in return, and then looked around the room. The scent of perfume from the various exotic shrubs that grew in planters around the walls was over-

powering, and Camilla used her interest in the plants to
relieve her nervousness.

'I've never seen so many different varieties of flowers!'
she exclaimed, addressing her remarks equally to
Alessandro and his servant, and Wong Lee's expression
grew animated.

'The *signore's* mother is a keen gardener,' he said,
spreading his arms as he had done before. 'She loves
creating beauty.' He shook his head. 'But I hear there
are many beautiful gardens in England. Do you have a
garden, Miss Richards?'

'Oh...' Camilla cast a diffident look in Alessandro's
direction, and then made a negative gesture '...no. No,
I'm afraid not. I...live in a flat, you see. A window-
box is the best that I can do.'

'A *flat*?'

Wong Lee seemed quite prepared to stand and debate
Camilla's circumstances, but his employer was growing
restless. 'She lives in an apartment, Lee,' he told the
little man rather testily. 'The English call them *flats*, for
some reason best known to themselves. Probably because they're all on one level. No stairs, you see.'

'Ah!' Enlightenment dawned, and Wong Lee smiled
again. But then, seeing that the other man was gazing
at him with a decided lack of tolerance, he quickly
stepped back and gestured towards long windows that
opened out on to a sunlit patio. 'Please, *signore*, sit. I
will tell Mama Lu you are...*both*...here.'

'Do that.'

Alessandro offered a tight smile, and then indicated
that Camilla should precede him outside. She did so a
little unwillingly, supremely conscious of him behind her,
observing the sway of her hips, the pale legs, emerging
from her shorts, that never tanned, no matter how long
she sat in the sun.

In an effort to maintain an appearance of composure,
however, she didn't hurry. Instead, as she sauntered
ahead of him, she made a leisurely appraisal of the pretty
garden-room, admiring the basketwork furniture that
was set at intervals between trellises of trailing vines, the
bright cushions that covered them adding generous
splashes of colour to the greenery.

She emerged on to a flagged terrace that spread in both directions and was liberally shaded by a frangipani-hung pergola. Bees buzzed among the fragrant blossoms, and the air was much gentler now, brushing her skin like warm silk. A table was waiting on the terrace, spread with a crisp white cloth and set for two. A jug of freshly squeezed orange juice, a steaming pot of coffee, and a plate of blueberry pancakes already resided on the table, together with butter on ice, a trio of preserves, and sweet maple syrup.

Camilla caught her breath and looked round at her host, but he was showing no particular interest in the waiting breakfast, and she quickly averted her head again. Obviously this was just a normal day for him, or at least as normal as it could be with his wife and daughter missing, but for Camilla it was all new and exciting. Even in the present situation there was an irresistible sense of anticipation to the day, and she didn't need to look at the ocean surging on to the beach only yards away to feel the blood quickening in her veins.

Alessandro Conti waited beside the table, and, realising he expected her to sit down so that he could take his own seat, she subsided on to one of the cushioned plastic chairs. It was superbly comfortable, but now was not the time to say so. Instead, she accepted the jug of orange juice he proffered, and made a creditable job of pouring some into the stemmed glass that stood by her plate.

'This... this is lovely,' she said at last, wiping a film of juice from her upper lip. 'Just like... just like...'

She had been going to say 'being on holiday', but the inappropriate words stuck in her throat, and instead she brought her glass to her lips again, trying desperately to think of an alternative.

'Like... being on holiday?' Alessandro suggested, a certain dryness to his tone, and Camilla managed to control her colour with a distinct effort.

'Well... yes,' she said, deciding there was no point in lying to him. 'This is a... heavenly spot.'

Alessandro inclined his head. 'I like it.'

'Oh, but surely, Virginia——' Camilla realised she had put her foot in it once again, and finished somewhat lamely, 'Virginia must, too.'

'No.' He was very definite about that. 'My...wife...finds Kumaru boring.'

'Kumaru.' Camilla liked the way he said it. Until then it had just been an address, but suddenly it had assumed an identity all its own.

'Yes, Kumaru,' replied Alessandro shortly, and she realised she must have spoken her thoughts aloud.

Mama Lu's arrival precluded any further discussion, and for once Camilla was relieved to see the house-keeper. In a long flowing gown that was patterned in exotic island colours, she came across the terrace towards them, her dark face split by a white-toothed smile. Camilla couldn't help wondering if she was remembering how she had had to put their guest to bed the night before, and whether she was comparing Camilla's skimpy body with her own generous curves. After all, there was no denying that, for all her size, Mama Lu swelled in all the right places. Fat she might be, but unshapely she was not.

'Is everything OK here?' she asked, and Alessandro glanced up at her, his expression gentling amazingly. If he had been attractive before the smile that tilted his rather thin lips now gave his face a startling sensitivity, and for all her staunch resistance Camilla felt an instinctive response.

Then he looked at her, and she pressed her palms down on her knees, under the level of the table, feeling their dampness against her legs. 'What do you want for breakfast, Miss Richards?' he enquired politely. 'Just say what you'd like, and Mama Lu will do the rest.'

'Oh...' Camilla surveyed the table, and then lifted her slim shoulders. 'I...generally just have coffee at home. This is fine, really. I'm not very hungry.'

Which wasn't strictly true. It was almost twenty-four hours since she had had a decent meal, and, although she didn't look as though she did, she had a fairly healthy appetite.

'Not hungry?' exclaimed Mama Lu now, clearly not believing her. 'But you had no supper!'

'I know.' Camilla gave her a rueful smile, hoping she was not going to make a big thing of that, and Mama Lu snorted.

'Don't you like pancakes?' she asked, a frown drawing her dark brows together, and, although Camilla was sure Alessandro Conti didn't allow the housekeeper to browbeat all his guests like this, she wasn't a *normal* visitor.

'I . . . love pancakes,' she replied defensively, and then caught her breath when the housekeeper picked up her plate and ladled a generous helping of the blueberry pancakes on to it. She smothered these with maple syrup, and then set the plate back in front of Camilla.

'Enjoy,' she said, pouring both her employer and his guest some coffee. 'And you let me know if you want any more.'

She ambled away again, and, while Camilla didn't expect her host to make any comment, he surprised her yet again. 'Leave them if you don't want them,' he said, eyeing her with mild amusement. 'Mama Lu thinks everyone should eat generously. It's her way of justifying her appearance.'

'Hmm.' Camilla acknowledged his explanation with a rueful grimace, but the smell of the pancakes was so delicious that she couldn't resist taking up her fork and trying them.

'So. . .' he said, after pouring himself more coffee, 'd'you want to tell me why you really came here?'

Camilla's mouth was full, and she had to empty it before she could speak. But his words were so disturbing that it was difficult to swallow the sticky pudding, and her eyes were watering by the time she was able to answer him.

'Why?' she squeaked, and then, clearing her throat, 'You know why. Virginia . . . Virginia invited me.'

'Yes. But why did she invite you?' Alessandro asked steadily. 'Why now? And why hasn't she mentioned you to me before?'

That hurt. It really did. She would have expected Virginia to have mentioned their friendship to Alessandro. If it had meant as much to Virginia as she

had always said then she should have talked about her
to her husband.

'I...don't know,' she said now, taking another
mouthful of the pancake almost automatically. 'I really
don't.'

'No.' Alessandro seemed to believe her, and she
breathed a little more easily. But then he spoiled it by
adding, 'And you didn't know she wouldn't be here when
you arrived?'

'No.' Camilla swallowed again, and forked another
mouthful of pancake into her mouth. 'Why would I?'
she demanded, her voice muffled by the food. 'I thought
she was happy here.'

'How do you know she wasn't?' he shot back at her,
and Camilla felt indignation at his attitude taking hold
of her.

'*You* said she was bored,' she reminded him in the
clear, concise tones she used in court, and now it was
his turn to look discomfited.

'Oh, yes,' he said ruefully, and her indignation dis-
solved in the face of his admission. 'I forgot.'

Camilla sighed. 'You've still no idea where they are,
then?' she asked, and he hesitated only a moment before
shaking his head. 'So...what are you going to do?'

He put down his napkin then, and got up from the
table, walking to the edge of the terrace and gazing out
towards the ocean. He was silent for so long that Camilla
thought he wasn't going to answer her, but then he
turned, with one hand gripping an arch of the pergola,
and said flatly, 'What do you think I should do?'

'Me?' Camilla said the word around another mouthful
of the pancakes. Despite her claims to the contrary, she
had known her appetite would not remain dormant and
she was embarrassed to discover that she had almost
emptied her plate. Putting down her fork, she used her
own napkin to dab her mouth, and then shrugged.
'Well—make enquiries, I suppose.'

'And where would you make those enquiries?'

'Where?' Camilla called upon her own experiences for
an answer. 'Um...well, do you know if they're still on
the island? Could they be visiting friends, or something——?'

'A woman and a child, answering my wife and daughter's description, left the island the same day they disappeared,' he told her bleakly. 'They flew to Los Angeles, on United Airlines, flight number——'

'You say a woman and a child answering your wife and daughter's description,' Camilla interrupted him quickly. 'Didn't they use their own names?'

Alessandro left the pergola and came back to the table. 'I'm afraid I have to go,' he said, without answering her. 'There are some phone calls I want to make, and then I'll be leaving for my office. You're welcome to stay here for a couple of days if you'd like to do so. But I suggest you make enquiries about your return flight to London. It isn't always easy to get a booking at this time of year. April through October is the busiest season, as I guess you found out at the airport.'

Camilla blinked. 'At the airport?' She was confused.

'When you tried to hire a car,' he explained, and her brows, which were a deeper, dark auburn shade, drew together.

'How do you know about that?'

Alessandro looked faintly rueful now, as if he regretted having said so much. 'I...saw you,' he said. And, as if justifying such a startling statement, he added, 'Your hair: it's quite...eye-catching.'

'You mean...you came to meet me? But I thought you said——'

'I didn't come to meet you,' retorted Alessandro quellingly. 'I flew back from Los Angeles on the same flight you did.'

'Los Angeles!' Camilla stared at him. 'So...you know where Virginia is!'

He was beginning to look a little irritable now, but he controlled his temper sufficiently to ask tersely, 'What makes you say that?'

Camilla's neck was beginning to ache with the effort of looking up at him, and, easing back her chair, she got rather jerkily to her feet. 'Well—you said a woman and a child answering your wife and daughter's description——'

'Oh, *that*!' He sighed then, and pushed long, impatient fingers through the thick dark hair that was

longer than Camilla normally liked. The gesture caused
his suit jacket to swing open, exposing the silvery grey
shirt beneath and the narrow slate-coloured tie that
matched it so flawlessly. It also drew Camilla's eyes to
his lean body, but she hastily averted them again. 'Yes,'
he went on, and she forced herself to look up. 'Virginia
and Maria—that's my daughter—did go to Los Angeles.
But I haven't seen them. Our investigation traced them
as far as San Diego, but after that—nothing.'

Camilla blinked. 'Your... investigation?'

'Yes.' Alessandro looked at her as if he resented this
invasion into his private affairs, but was obliged to continue. 'You didn't think I'd let Virginia get away with
this, did you?'

Camilla didn't know what to think. What exactly had
Virginia got away with? And why would her husband
employ a private investigator to find her? Surely, sooner
or later, she was bound to get in touch.

'I have to go,' he said now, fastening the single button
on the jacket over his flat stomach. 'As I said, you're
welcome to stay on for a few days, if that's what you
want to do. But I'm afraid I'm going to be too busy to
entertain you.'

The detached impersonality of his tone was not encouraging. Indeed, Camilla felt like nothing so much as
to tell him she would be leaving that morning, and be
done with Alessandro Conti once and for all. What
stopped her was the certain knowledge that that was what
he would like her to do, and, while she had no great
faith in Virginia either, she had flown a hell of a long
way just to be told she should turn round and go home
again.

So, instead of responding to his remarks in the way
he wanted, she forced a polite smile and said, 'I don't
need entertaining, Mr Conti. I'm sure I'll find plenty to
do to fill my time, and it does seem a shame to leave
without giving Virginia a chance to get in touch with
me.'

CHAPTER FOUR

THAT stopped Alessandro in his tracks. He had reached the glass door that led into the house, and Camilla guessed he had expected to have the last word. But now he paused, gripping the frame of the door with one hand, as he allowed what she had said to turn over in his mind.

He had nice hands, she found herself thinking, the slim, leather-strapped gold watch he wore drawing her attention to the dark hairs on the wrist that protruded from his cuff. He wore a wedding ring, too, on his third finger, but no other jewellery, she noticed. Indeed, for a man of his wealth and affluence, his needs appeared to be remarkably conservative. But then, she concluded ruefully, a man like Alessandro Conti didn't need to broadcast his superiority. Without any of the accoutrements that money had brought him, he would still be a man to be reckoned with.

'You could be right,' he said now, but slowly; reluctantly, she suspected. 'Virginia might try to get in touch with you.' He considered this possibility, and then pressed his balled fist against the window-frame. 'Do I have your assurance that, if she does, you'll tell me?'

Camilla hesitated. 'You mean... even if she doesn't want me to?'

His thin yet sensual lips twitched. 'That's exactly what I mean, Miss Richards.'

She took a deep breath. 'And if I say no, you'll find some reason for me to leave here sooner, rather than later, right?'

His nostrils flared. 'No,' he said, but there was an edge of hostility to his voice now. 'I would not be so discourteous, Miss Richards. However, I have to say that if I find you've been lying to me——'

'I haven't been lying to you!' Camilla found her nerve was not as great as she had thought. 'For goodness' sake,

I've told you everything I know.' Well, almost everything. 'I don't know what's going on, any more than you apparently do.'

'Apparently?' He hadn't missed the qualification, and she felt the hot colour bathing first her throat and then her face with scarlet.

'Well, I don't know you, do I?' she protested defensively. 'I—I mean…you could have something to do with Virginia's disappearance, for all I know!'

She expected an explosion then. Her reckless words, brought about by a need to justify her own position, exposed the true state of her feelings towards him, and she was quite prepared for Alessandro to respond in kind.

But, instead, a faintly weary expression crossed his face and, shaking his head, he straightened. 'Of course,' he said, as if she hadn't just accused him of being implicated in his wife's disappearance. 'As you say, we are strangers. And you have every right to form your own opinion of the situation. All I can say in my own defence is that Virginia has never had anything to fear from me. On the contrary, had that been so this farce of a marriage would not have survived six months, let alone six years!'

The sun was hot on her shoulders, but Camilla hardly noticed it. She had noticed the heat of the sand beneath her feet, but that was because she had taken off her canvas boots, and the shifting sand between her toes was unfamiliar. Occasionally she bent and rescued a shell from her path, but even the beauty of cowrie and conch was only of passing interest. Her real attention was concentrated on more personal matters, particularly the not wholly unexpected announcement that Virginia's marriage was on the rocks.

Of course, Virginia's letter had implied as much, and her running away indicated a depth of desperation Camilla had yet to come to terms with. But what she couldn't understand was why her friend and her husband hadn't simply got a divorce when it seemed obvious that they both resented the ties that bound them together. After all, divorce was so easy in the United States. A simple trip to Nevada, or some other state where the divorce laws could be manipulated, and you were free again. Ready to make the same mistakes again, thought Camilla ruefully. Perhaps being independent wasn't such a bad thing after all.

Still, this wasn't the time to be considering her own principles. Just because no man had ever lived up to her expectations was no reason to apply her precepts to this situation. And, if she was perfectly honest, she would have to admit that not all the men she had rejected had wanted her. Her job frightened off the less intellectual among them, and not everyone liked hair that defied all her efforts to tone it down.

Which brought Alessandro Conti to mind again. The moment when she had challenged his admission of seeing her at the airport had been the only time when she had come close to truly disconcerting him. Oh, he had been roused by her suggestion that Virginia might try to get in touch with her; but only when she had picked up on his evaluation of her conversation with the girl at the car rentals desk had he shown any trace of embarrassment. He had not liked admitting that he had noticed her, even if it was her hair that had provoked his interest. It was as if he resented showing any kind of weakness, and Camilla wondered if he had always been that way. It might even provide part of the reason why Virginia had run away. If she had tried to get close to him, but he hadn't let her.

Camilla felt a prickling of gooseflesh over her skin. She wasn't cold; how could she be in this climate? But something had sent a sense of chill over her bones, and it wasn't the temperature. For a moment she was quite cold, and then it dispersed again, and she breathed more easily. Someone must have walked over her grave, she thought impatiently, recalling what her godmother had used to say on occasions like that. Either that, or she had imagined the whole thing.

She came to a standstill and tipped her head back on her shoulders, allowing the heat of the sun to beat against her closed eyelids. How could anybody be unhappy here? she wondered, opening her eyes again and blinking at the view. Yards and yards of unblemished sand stretched in either direction, and, behind her, tall palms raised their branches to the blue, blue sky. Apart from a few seabirds she had the beach to herself, and, while she knew that that was because this whole promontory belonged to Alessandro Conti, she still found it amazing.

She dropped her boots on to the sand and walked down to the water's edge. Although she knew the water was warm, its initial feel was cold, and she retreated as a creaming breaker splintered on the sand at her feet. But its attraction was irresistible, and she half wished she had put her swim-suit on under her shorts.

And then she sighed, and went back to pick up her boots again. She wasn't here to have fun, she reminded herself severely. She had come in answer to Virginia's summons, and just because she wasn't here—no, *particularly* because she wasn't here—she ought to be considering what she could do to help, instead of paddling in the ocean.

The trouble was, she didn't know what she could do. Alessandro seemed to have everything in hand, and if he couldn't find his wife how could she expect to do so? It wasn't as if these were familiar surroundings for her. She hadn't even been all that confident about hiring a car, whatever Alessandro had thought to the contrary. Only Virginia had suggested in her letter that Camilla might pretend to be touring the island, and call at the Conti estate as if by chance.

That it hadn't happened that way was probably just as well, in the circumstances. And, when Camilla had discovered she needed an international driving licence to hire a car, she hadn't hesitated before hiring a taxi to bring her to Kumaru. She had been worried about her friend, and with good reason as it turned out.

It seemed further, walking back to the house, than she had thought. Or perhaps it was just that she was still tired. And although there was a breeze it was still very hot, and she simply wasn't used to the enervating effects of the heat. Unlike Alessandro, she thought, his lean dark features coming rather too easily to mind. The heat didn't seem to bother him, and this morning he had looked every bit as cool and businesslike as any of the partners in her office back home. Alessandro...

She cut her thoughts off there. She was getting far too
accustomed to thinking of him by his first name. If she
wasn't careful she'd use it when she was speaking to him,
and that would be really embarrassing. It would be different if Virginia were here and she had introduced them.
As it was they had no point of contact, and calling him
Alessandro seemed too familiar.

Of course, it shouldn't be, she argued as she climbed
the steps to the terrace. The Americans she had met had
been generally friendly, and not at all formal. But these
were not usual circumstances, she admitted ruefully.
And, until Virginia was found, she had the feeling she
and Virginia's husband would remain on opposite sides
of an invisible fence.

The stone terrace was hot beneath her feet, and she
was bending to put her boots on again when she sensed
other eyes upon her. She straightened and looked about
her but the terrace was deserted, and she frowned. Then,
instinctively, she tilted her head. A man was standing
on the balcony above. She guessed access to the balcony
must be gained through one of the living-rooms on the
main floor, and she couldn't help wondering how long
he had been standing there, watching her.

However, the man seemed not at all disconcerted by
her observation of him. He still leaned on the balcony,
arms spread, the sleeves of the pale blue shirt he was
wearing rolled above his elbows. 'Hi,' he said, inclining
his head in her direction. 'Enjoy your walk?'

The sun was bright in her eyes, and, unable to sustain
his smiling gaze, Camilla averted her head. 'Yes. Very
much,' she replied, limiting her curiosity to an oc-
casional darting glance. Who was he? she wondered. And
what was he doing here?

'You must be . . . Camilla, right?' he declared, folding
his arms together and bending until he was resting his
chin on his wrists. 'Are you coming up?'

In spite of her earlier ambivalence at the lack of informality, Camilla found she resented the familiar way
he used her name. After all, he hadn't even told her who
he was, and the look she cast up at him was not
encouraging.

'Perhaps,' she responded now, completing the fastening of her boots but making no rush to do so. Instead, she lingered for several minutes after she had finished, just staring at the view, before turning, reluctantly, in the direction of the house.

He didn't speak to her again, but he was waiting at the top of the half-spiral staircase when she reached the landing. 'At last,' he said without rancour, a half-smile playing about his lips. 'Let's go into the living-room. I've asked Mama Lu to bring us some coffee.'

Camilla gave him another uncompromising stare, but she accompanied him across the hall and into the high-ceilinged room that gave on to the balcony she had seen from below. It was a room she hadn't entered before, but that was hardly surprising, she acknowledged. Apart from the parlour, where she had met Alessandro the previous afternoon, and her own bedroom, of course, she was unfamiliar with the house, but she made no comment as she followed him inside.

Her immediate impression was one of light, and comfort, and superb decoration. The patio doors, which opened on to the balcony, were closed now, allowing the air-conditioning to work unhindered, and Camilla appreciated the change of temperature. It had been so hot outside, but in here it was refreshingly cool.

She stood on an enormous circular carpet that was patterned in muted jewel-like colours, looking at long, inviting sofas made of squashy cream leather. There were oases of smaller chairs and tables, with flowers set in vases, and exotic oriental bowls, and lots of pictures on walls that were otherwise quite plain. It was a lovely room, Camilla thought; a family room; and, as if to emphasise the point, an exquisite doll's house stood in one corner, with a row of dolls propped on the floor beside it.

It was the first indication she had seen of the child she had previously only heard of, and Camilla knew an instinctive feeling of remorse. She would have liked to have met Virginia's daughter, she thought ruefully. She pondered who she was most like: her mother, or her father?

'I guess you're wondering who I am,' the man said now, and although she was tempted to deny it Camilla looked at him and raised enquiring eyebrows. 'The name's Grant Blaisdell,' he went on, exhibiting the kind of brash self-confidence that Camilla had always found most tedious. 'Alex's cousin.'

'Al ... Mr Conti's *cousin*!'

Heavens, she thought, she never would have guessed. Although both men were tall and broad-shouldered, there was no family resemblance that she could see. Grant Blaisdell was fair, whereas Alessandro was dark; his eyes were blue, whereas Alessandro's were brown; and his softer, admittedly more handsome features lacked the harsh masculinity of his cousin's.

'*Mr* Conti!' he was saying disparagingly now, not giving Camilla time to worry about the fact that she seemed to have studied Alessandro's face rather too thoroughly, and she lifted her slim shoulders in a dismissing gesture. 'Don't tell me you call him *Mr* Conti! I thought Ginny was a friend of yours.'

'Ginny? Oh, you mean Virginia.' Camilla could be excessively pedantic when she chose. 'Yes. We are friends. But Mr Conti and I had never met before yesterday.'

'No kidding?' Grant Blaisdell was unimpressed. 'Well, why don't we sit down and talk about it? That way you can tell me when you last saw ... Virginia.'

Camilla hesitated, but she was tired, and the sofas looked very appealing. However, she eschewed their comfort in favour of one of the smaller armchairs, thus preventing Grant Blaisdell from sitting too close beside her.

She suspected he recognised the ploy, but he made no comment. Instead, he seated himself in another of the armchairs, and when Wong Lee arrived with the tray of coffee he was obliged to set it on the inlaid chest that stood near by.

'Would you like me to pour the coffee, *signora*?' he asked, looking at Camilla and not at his employer's cousin, and she took a moment to appreciate the fact.

'We can do it, Lee,' Grant declared, dismissing him, but Wong Lee didn't move.

'I...yes...that's all right, Mr Wong,' Camilla agreed quickly. 'Thank you.'

'Thank you, *signora*; *signore*.'

The latter was said almost as an afterthought, but Grant didn't look put out. 'I guess Lee and I aren't the best of friends,' he remarked, waiting rather impatiently for Camilla to pour his coffee. Then, 'Thanks. No one makes better coffee than Mama Lu. Don't you think so?'

Camilla shook her head, still absorbing the fact that Wong Lee had deferred to her and not Grant. 'I don't suppose I'm as familiar with it as you are,' she murmured after a moment, and Grant gave a snort of agreement.

'Oh, right,' he said. 'You're English, aren't you? I guess you prefer tea to coffee, yeah?' He grimaced. 'I don't blame you. I've never met an English person who could make a half-decent cup of coffee anyway.'

Camilla sat back in her chair, taking her cup of coffee with her, wondering how one man could be so insensitive without apparently being aware of it. How could he sit here, discussing the merits of tea or coffee, when his cousin's wife was missing, and he hadn't even said he was sorry?

'So,' he continued, evidently unable to sit silent for long, even though he was munching his way through the assortment of biscuits Mama Lu had added to the tray, 'how well do you know Gi...Virginia?'

Camilla pressed her mouth closed. 'We went to school together.'

'You did?' He sounded surprised, and she wondered why. 'I'd have said you were a good five years younger.'

'Oh.' Camilla should have recognised the line when she heard it, but her mind had been diverted by his question. 'Well, we're the same age,' she replied evenly. 'Sorry to disappoint you.'

'Hey, it's no disappointment.' Grant's eyes were annoyingly intent. 'Women are like wine, I always say: the older the year, the better the vintage.'

Oh, really! Camilla didn't say the words out loud, but she wanted to. She couldn't believe she was sitting here, listening to such a load of drivel, and she wished he would get to the point of his visit—if he had one.

'Mr Conti—that is, your cousin—is not here, you know,' she volunteered steadily. 'I believe he said he was going to his office. If you want to see him——'

'Sure. I'll see Alex later.' Grant leaned across to pour himself more coffee, and she noticed, with distaste, the circle of sweat that dampened his shirt beneath his arm. She was surprised, too. It was still fairly early in the day, and if Grant had come here by car—which seemed reasonably certain—he was bound to have been sitting in an air-conditioned atmosphere for most of the morning. And yet...

She shrugged. It was of no interest to her anyway. Grant Blaisdell was of no interest to her. She knew plenty of men like him in London, and she had never been attracted by their unsubtle initiatives.

'Alex and I work together,' Grant was explaining now. 'His father and my mother are brother and sister, so we both have a stake in the Conti Corporation's future.'

'I see.'

Camilla wasn't interested in his relationship to his cousin, but she had to admit that anything that concerned Alessandro—*Alex*... she tried the name out on her tongue, and found she liked it very much—anything concerning Alex did intrigue her.

'I run the place when he's away,' Grant added expansively. 'I guess you could say I'm his vice-president.' He laughed suddenly. 'Yes, I think that describes my position very well.' His face sobered. 'What do you think?'

Camilla shook her head. 'I'm sure you know your own worth best, Mr Blaisdell,' she responded coolly. 'I'm afraid I couldn't comment.'

'*Mr* Blaisdell!' Happily, her use of his surname diverted him from any closer examination of her words. 'The name's Grant, Camilla. I don't believe in wasting time with formalities. Any friend of Ginny's is a friend of mine. Didn't she ever mention me to you?'

'No.' Camilla finished her coffee and bent forward to replace the cup on the tray. 'It's...some years since we were last in touch.'

'But she wrote to you, didn't she?' Grant had leaned forward too, and when Camilla would have drawn back his fingers curled about her forearm. 'When I phoned Alex last night he said she'd invited you here.'

'That's right.'

Camilla answered him, but her eyes were dark with anger at his presumption, and, as if realising he was being too intense, he released her again. He spread both hands then, palms outward, towards her, and gave a rueful little grimace as if begging her indulgence.

'I'm sorry, I'm sorry. But we're all pretty desperate to know where she is,' he excused himself. 'And…Maria, of course. It's a bloody situation, and we're all worried sick!'

'Mmm.' Camilla made the required sound of endorsement, but she couldn't help thinking that Grant Blaisdell's sympathy had come a little late. She had the feeling that he was unlikely to worry about anything that didn't affect him directly, and if she was being uncharitable she couldn't help it. She didn't like him. She didn't know why, but she just had a gut feeling about him. It was probably due to the fact that she resented anyone treating her as a sexual target first, and a woman second.

'Well…' Evidently he had decided it was time he was leaving, and he pressed down on the arms of his chair and got to his feet. 'I'd like nothing better than to spend the rest of the morning here with you, but I guess I ought to at least show my face downtown. It's been a real pleasure meeting you, Camilla, and if you're spending any time on the island perhaps we can get together again real soon.'

Camilla looked up at him, her face composed into a polite mask, but she didn't say anything to encourage his attentions. 'Goodbye, Mr Blaisdell,' she said, making no move to get out of her chair, and, with a final considering appraisal, he nodded his head and left her.

After he had gone, Camilla waited until she heard the unmistakable sound of a car's engine before getting out of her seat. Then, when she did get up, she stood for a moment with her arms crossed over her midriff, rubbing her elbows with the palms of her hands. It was a defensive gesture, and she didn't really know why she should feel that way; but she did. She was glad he had gone, and she hoped she would not have to see him again before she left the island.

And yet he had said he was a friend of Virginia's, or words to that effect anyway. Perhaps she should have asked him where he thought her friend had gone. He was probably party to any information Alex had. *Alex.* She tried his name again, and decided it was a lot easier to handle than Alessandro. Whatever, he was bound to have kept his own family in touch with any developments. And, while she suspected she knew as much as he did about Virginia's current whereabouts, Grant might have been willing to speculate about her reasons for running away.

Mama Lu's appearance, ostensibly to collect the tray, interrupted this train of thought, and, feeling obliged to say something, Camilla thanked her for the coffee.

'Mr Grant's gone, then, has he?' the housekeeper responded, bending to pick up the tray, but Camilla guessed Mama Lu knew exactly when he had left the house.

However, 'Yes,' she answered, pushing her hands into the pockets of her shorts. 'About five minutes ago.'

'Mmm.' The housekeeper straightened, the tray in her hands. 'I thought so.'

Camilla's tongue came to moisten her lips. 'You—er— I suppose you know the family very well,' she ventured, and Mama Lu nodded, her dark head bobbing affirmatively.

'As well as I know my own,' she agreed, evidently more prepared to be friendly today. 'I've been around since before Vito and Sophia got married.'

'Vito...and Sophia?' Camilla frowned. 'Would that be—Mr Conti's father and mother?'

'His father and his *aunt*,' corrected Mama Lu patiently. 'Miss Sophia is Mr Grant's mother.'

'Oh, I see.' Camilla acknowledged her mistake. 'So...Mr Blaisdell is Mr Conti's cousin.'

'Did you doubt it?' The housekeeper arched dark brows, and Camilla was hard-pressed not to abandon this conversation here and now. But desperation drove her on.

'He just seems...so different from...from his cousin,' she murmured lamely, and Mama Lu shrugged.

'Isn't that the truth?' She lifted her fleshy shoulders. 'I guess he's more like his daddy than Miss Sophia thought.'

'His daddy?' Camilla knew she was being unbearably nosy, but she couldn't stop now. 'Do—er—do his parents live on Oahu, too?'

'His mommy does,' replied Mama Lu, adjusting the cups on the tray. 'No one knows exactly where his daddy is.'

'Oh. Oh, I see.'

'Cal Blaisdell left his wife and son when Grant was little more than a baby,' the housekeeper explained indifferently. 'Only married her 'cause he thought he'd inherit her daddy's business. But Alex's granddaddy died, leaving all his stock to Vito. Kinda sudden it was, and I guess he didn't have the time to include Cal in his will.'

Camilla's lips parted. She had the feeling she was getting into matters that didn't concern her. But it seemed that Mama Lu had no great love for the Blaisdells, and that was reassuring.

'What time would you like lunch?' the housekeeper asked now, and Camilla was relieved at the change of topic.

'Um...when...whenever it's convenient,' she murmured, lifting her shoulders. 'I don't want to put you to any trouble——'

'It's no trouble.' Mama Lu started towards the door, and then turned back. 'You staying for a while?'

'I...don't know.' Camilla didn't have an answer for her. 'For a couple of days, maybe.'

'You looking for Virginia, too?'

'You could say that.' Camilla shrugged. 'As I told you yesterday, I thought she'd be here.'

'Mmm.' Mama Lu absorbed this. 'Well, Alex will find her, if anyone can.'

'You think so?'

'I think so,' Mama Lu conceded. 'He wants that little girl back.'

'Little girl?' Camilla frowned. 'Oh—you mean...
Maria.'

'That's what I said,' agreed the housekeeper, wad-
dling out of the room. 'She made a mistake, taking the
little one with her. Alex won't rest until he finds her,
and then...'

But the rest of her sentence was made inaudible by
the fact that she was too far away for Camilla to hear
her, and she was left with the undoubted belief that
Virginia had made a bad enemy.

CHAPTER FIVE

ALEX was not alone when Camilla joined him for supper that evening.

She had spent the afternoon surreptitiously familiarising herself with the layout of the house, and when Mama Lu came to inform her that she was expected to join her host in the library at eight o'clock she had no difficulty in locating her destination. It was one of the rooms on the main floor whose windows overlooked the lawns at the side of the house, and she had already admired his collection of books.

She had discovered that, contrary to her belief, Alex and Virginia did not occupy the master suite of rooms. At lunch she had explained to Mama Lu how she had lost herself that morning, and, when she'd mentioned having seen Alex, the housekeeper had told her that the doors she had seen led into the south wing. Apparently Alex's father had had the wing added to the house when his son and Virginia got married, and although his parents no longer lived here the younger Contis still occupied their original apartments.

'I dare say Virginia would have preferred to move into the main apartments,' Mama Lu had conceded, as she'd served her guest crayfish salad and a lemon sorbet in the coolness of the dining-room, and once again Camilla had been left with the distinct impression that her friend had not endeared herself to the servants.

After lunch it was fairly easy to explore her surroundings. No one was around to disturb her wanderings, and she soon determined how to find her own room, and with that developed a passing recognition for the various halls and corridors. Once she had a point of contact she drew a mental picture of where she was in relation to the principal apartments, and for the time being that was enough.

She would have liked to have explored outside, but she decided that that would have to wait until another day—if she was still here. The sight of what looked like a stable block, half hidden among the trees, was intriguing, and there were horses grazing in a paddock that were visible from the windows of the parlour. But for now she decided not to overstep her welcome. Besides, there were security men in the grounds, and she had no wish to tangle with them again.

She was considering if she might be excused from joining her host for the evening meal when Mama Lu came to give her his message. Camilla had heard the sound of a car as she had sat on her balcony, enjoying the subtle shades that the setting sun painted on the eastern sky, and, although she had had no reason to feel so, a shiver of anticipation had rippled along her spine. If Grant Blaisdell aroused feelings of negativity inside her, his cousin did just the opposite, and it was disturbing to feel this awareness of a man who was not only married to her friend, but out of her league altogether. That was why she was hoping she might avoid another tête-à-tête with him. It wouldn't do for her to get involved, however singular that involvement might be.

But, receiving his invitation from the housekeeper, she knew she couldn't refuse to join him. After all, this was his house, and she was only here because he was allowing her to be so. The very idea of declining to have any contact with him was simply not feasible. And besides, she was curious to know if he had learned anything during the day.

However, deciding what to wear was another matter. Bearing in mind that she had bought her ticket for Hawaii at a moment's notice, she had had little time to update her wardrobe. Indeed, the clothes she had brought with her had all been acquired for other holidays, when informality had been the key.

Nevertheless, after some consideration she realised it would probably be unwise to dress up for the occasion. Better to dress down than to risk having her host think she was making some kind of play for his attention. That was the last thing she wanted to do, particularly in the present circumstances.

A jade-green chiffon blouse, teamed with black
culottes that were cut off in mid-calf, seemed an in-
nocuous combination. They were sufficiently smart
without being excessively formal, and if she liked the
way the feminine collar of the blouse contrasted with
her coil of red hair that was just an incidental bonus.
She had washed her hair again and smothered it with
conditioner, so that now it looked fairly secure in its
knot with only a few wisps of silk brushing her cheeks.
Dull gold rings gave a touch of sophistication to her ears,
but otherwise she wore no jewellery.

The heels of her shoes made an intermittent sound as
she stepped from the rugs that were spread along the
corridors to the polished floors between. It was an annoying adjunct to the accelerated beat of her heart, and
she tried to apply herself to the deep-breathing exercises
she normally practised before going into court. The
witness for the defence, she thought ruefully. She had
never realised how daunting that could be.

The doors to the library were open, and she heard the
voices, though not what they were saying, before she
reached her destination. Although her heart lifted at the
possibility that Virginia might be back, she didn't think
the voices were familiar, and when she halted in the
doorway her suppositions were confirmed. The man and
woman who were standing on either side of Alex Conti
were strangers to her, but although she hadn't seen them
before she thought she could guess who they must be.
The man was so like Alex—but older—that he had to
be his father; and, although the woman was smaller, and
less obviously related, her eyes mirrored those of her
son.

Alex saw her first. His guests were looking at him as
she appeared in the doorway, but he wasn't looking at
either of them. His head was bent as he appeared to be
listening to what his father was saying, but Camilla had
the feeling his attention was distracted. His expression
was curiously blank, and only when his eyes met
Camilla's did his face reveal any animation. Immediately there was a darkening of emotion between his narrowed lids, and a deepening of the lines around his
mouth.

She was not the only one to notice his changing expression however. Although his father still went on speaking, his mother was obviously more attuned to her son's feelings. Her head turned almost simultaneously, and it was her half-impatient, 'Vito!' that brought an end to their conversation.

Camilla, who had thought she was beyond the stage of blushing, now found it incredibly difficult to control the blood that rushed to the surface of her skin. With all three of them looking at her with varying degrees of curiosity, it wasn't easy to step into the room as if she had a right to be there. She didn't have that right. More and more she was convinced of it. Whatever Virginia's reasons for inviting her here, they were no longer valid.

'It's . . . Camilla, isn't it?' The woman standing beside Alex came forward to break the awkward silence that had fallen. She offered her hand in a friendly fashion. 'I'm Sonya Conti, Alex's mother. I don't believe we've ever met.'

'How do you do?' Camilla shook the other woman's hand with some relief. 'No. We've never met. I'm afraid I was away when . . . when Virginia and . . . your son got married.'

Sonya nodded, studying Camilla closely, but not in a hostile way. She appeared to accept what Camilla had told her, and the smile that lifted her lips was reassuring.

'So Alex told us,' she said, glancing round at her son and her husband. 'This is Alex's father, of course. Vito, come and say hello to Camilla.'

Vito Conti's hair was grey, and he had more flesh about his face and body than Alex had, but otherwise he was very like his son. Or, Camilla amended ruefully, she should say that Alex was like his father. Certainly, the family resemblance was a striking one.

He came now to take Camilla's hand, his expression less forgiving than his wife's. Evidently Alex's father was not prepared to take everything at face value, and although his greeting was polite it lacked warmth.

'Alex says you and Virginia went to school together,' he remarked, pushing his hands into the jacket pockets of the cream silk suit he was wearing. 'Where exactly was that?'

'Vito...'

His wife sounded horrified at the baldness of the question, but Camilla thought she could understand his reasoning. 'Queen Catherine's,' she answered at once, realising that any hesitation on her part could be misinterpreted. 'In Hertfordshire.'

'Hertfordshire?' Vito Conti frowned. 'Is that a place?'

'It's a county, Papa,' put in Alex abruptly. 'You know: they don't have states, they have counties. Hertfordshire is near London.'

'Is it?' His father didn't sound convinced. 'But you must have left school some...ten years ago, no?'

'Eleven actually,' confirmed Camilla, her colour rising in spite of herself, and Alex expelled his breath on a heavy sigh.

'Miss Richards doesn't know where Virginia is, Papa,' he said flatly, emptying the glass he had held cradled in his hand. He looked at her as he finished his drink, and inclined his head politely. 'Can I get you something, Miss Richards? A Martini; or a cocktail, perhaps——?'

'For goodness' sake!' Sonya intervened once again. 'Why do you call her Miss Richards, Alex? She is...Virginia's friend. Can't you address her by her given name? I'm sure Camilla would prefer it.'

Camilla nodded. 'I would.' She moistened her lips. 'And...I'd prefer a glass of white wine if you have one—um—Alex.'

It was a rash move, but at least it removed the fear of using his name unthinkingly. And, although one brow quirked a little, he didn't object. Though how could he, she argued silently, with his mother championing her cause, and making an effort to be friendly?

With a glass of chilled Chablis in her hand, she felt a little less under siege. The wine was delicious, and it gave her something to do with her hands. It also gave her something to hide behind when eyes were turned in her direction—and a useful delaying tactic if a question was too personal.

'And have you seen my daughter-in-law since you left school?' Vito queried, letting it be known that he for one was not prepared to let the subject drop.

Camilla nodded. 'Of course. We've ... kept in touch.'
Or was that totally honest? Did two meetings and a
wedding invitation constitute 'keeping in touch'? She
didn't have the answer. But then, nor did he.

'You wrote to one another?'

Vito was like a dog at a bone, and his son gave him
an impatient look. 'Does it matter?' he demanded. 'If
Virginia kept in touch with one person or one thousand,
would that give us any clue to her whereabouts? I've
told you: Camilla...' he said the name almost exper-
imentally '...Camilla doesn't know any more than we
do. Give us all a break, will you? When Morales has
some news he'll let us know.'

His father looked as if he would have liked to argue,
but his wife evidently endorsed her son's statement, and
he gave a resigned shrug of his shoulders. It was obvious
that they both shared their son's anxiety. They just had
different ways of showing it.

'Come,' said Sonya, patting Camilla's arm now, 'let's
sit down and enjoy our aperitif.' She led the way to where
two padded velvet armchairs formed part of an intimate
grouping. 'You must tell us what you think of our island.
Is this your first visit to Hawaii?'

Although Camilla would have preferred to stand, she
was obliged to accept her hostess's invitation. But she
was intensely conscious of both Alex and his father
watching their tête-à-tête and she guessed that, in her
way, Sonya was every bit as inquisitive as her husband.

Still, for the moment she could speak frankly about
her first impressions of Oahu. It was easier speaking of
impersonal things, and she knew she went on too long
in an effort to avoid further questions.

Behind her she was conscious of Alex pouring himself
and his father another drink—Scotch, she thought,
judging by the faint aroma of malt that drifted to her
nostrils—and returning to prop his hips against the
leather-topped desk that occupied the space beside the
windows. Like his father, he was wearing a suit of some
lightweight material, but the colour was dark, sombre,
a fitting adjunct to the sombre cast of his features.

It was dark outside, but the curtains had not yet been
drawn, and a moth came to beat its wings against the

glass. In the lamplit room there should have been peace and tranquillity, but there wasn't. They were all on edge, for various reasons, and although Camilla knew she should have sympathy with her friend she wondered how Virginia could justify what she had done.

As well as the books, which lined two of the walls from floor to ceiling, the room contained a collection of chess sets, some of them behind glass. There were also several items of artistic merit, including one or two sculptures, which even Camilla recognised as collector's pieces, and an ancient map of the western world that Vasco de Gama would have found invaluable.

Yet, like the living-room Camilla had seen earlier, the room was first and foremost what it claimed to be: an attractive library cum study, with a pile of official-looking documents on the desk signifying someone's efforts to work here. Like all the rooms in the house, it was meant to be used and enjoyed, not revered, though whether Virginia would have seen it that way Camilla couldn't be sure. It was hard to be objective, but her memories of Virginia were of someone who wanted her share of the good things in life; who enjoyed spending money, and was prepared to marry anyone who could sustain that kind of lifestyle. But whether that lifestyle could be adjusted to include being a wife and mother was something else.

'And you are not married?' Sonya queried swiftly when she ran out of things to say, and Camilla shook her head.

'No.'

'So... you are a career woman.' Sonya's smile was enquiring, as well as sympathetic. 'A model, perhaps?'

'Oh, no.' Camilla made a negative gesture, aware that their conversation was being monitored by Virginia's husband and his father. 'I—er—I'm a solicitor, actually.'

'A solicitor?' Vito left his son, and came to stand in front of her. 'A lawyer? Virginia's lawyer, perhaps, hmm?'

'I'm afraid not.' Camilla looked up at him frankly, and the old man lifted his shoulders.

'But you could be.'

'I don't think so. I . . . well, I'm not allowed to practise in the United States. And besides, I don't deal in——'

She broke off abruptly, realising she had been about to say 'divorce', and wishing she had never started this. They didn't know she had any reason to assume that Virginia might want a divorce. And indeed, for all her claims against her husband, Virginia hadn't mentioned divorce in her letter.

'You don't deal in—what, Miss Richards?' Alex had taken up where his father had left off, and she looked up into his dark face with real discomfort. He had been defending her. Now he was gazing at her as if all his previous suspicions about her had suddenly been confirmed. He drew a breath. 'Blackmail, perhaps?'

'*Blackmail!*'

'*Alex!*'

Camilla and his mother spoke simultaneously, and Camilla's astonishment was so genuine that no one could believe she had faked it. Least of all Alex, she realised weakly, as, with a gesture of apology at his mother's indignation, he moved away.

But it had given her something to think about, something she had hitherto not considered. It seemed unbelievable, but Alex evidently thought Virginia's actions were calculated. That she had taken his daughter away to gain some cardinal advantage.

The arrival of Wong Lee to announce that supper was ready was quite a relief. Not that Camilla believed she could escape questioning over the food. On the contrary, sitting at the table there would be no chance to avoid being scrutinised like a specimen on a pin. But it did mean that soon the meal would be over. And when it was she intended to excuse herself forthwith.

Mama Lu seemed to have put her own feelings aside in an effort to create an aura of normality, and the table in the dining-room reflected her diligence. Fine crystal and silver were reflected in the polished mahogany of its surface, and a centre-piece of mauve orchids and scarlet hibiscus was lit by a pair of candelabra that provided the only illumination. It was like a scene from a film, Camilla reflected, trying not to flinch away from Alex's fingers as he held her chair for her. She hadn't really believed people actually lived like this, but, from the way her host and his parents accepted the situation, it was obviously no novelty to them.

The food was equally superlative. Fresh pineapple, which Sonya told her grew in great profusion all over the island, was served with wafer-thin slices of smoked ham. This was followed by a creamy seafood fricassee, and to finish there was more of the delicious Columbian coffee, with fruit and cheese.

Everything was perfect, but Camilla noticed that no one really did justice to the food. She also noticed that Alex drank steadily throughout the meal, continually re-filling his glass from the several bottles of chilled white Burgundy that Wong Lee provided. Yet he didn't appear to suffer any effects from the alcohol, and for once he didn't respond to the reproving looks his mother kept sending in his direction. Only his eyes revealed any emotion, and that a guarded impatience, occasionally pointed towards herself.

For herself, she ate sparingly, and limited herself to only two glasses of wine. She wasn't used to drinking much at all, and she had no wish to weaken what little defence she had. Instead, she concentrated on moving the food round her plate, and listened to what Alex's parents had to say.

It was obvious no progress had been made in discovering Virginia's and Maria's whereabouts, and once during the meal Sonya's voice broke as she spoke about her granddaughter.

'I pray to God Virginia is looking after her!' she exclaimed, crossing herself in the age-old religious gesture of faith. 'He knows she seldom showed any interest in the child when she was here.'

She groped for her handbag, and, extracting a tissue, blew her nose rather forcefully, and her husband reached across the table to pat her hand. 'Courage, Sonya,' he said gently, and, meeting Alex's eyes across his parents' gaze, Camilla felt a shuddering impact in her heart.

Because his wife was upset, Alex's father pre-empted Camilla's intention to excuse herself after supper. As soon as they left the table, Vito declared that he and Sonya were leaving. 'It's late,' he said, although it was only a little after ten o'clock. 'And your mother's tired. Come by tomorrow, and we'll talk again. I have some ideas, but they can wait until morning.'

Alex inclined his head. 'OK,' he said, and Camilla hung back as he accompanied his parents into the entrance hall. 'We'll find her, Mama, and Maria. As God is my witness, I'll never give up.'

Camilla was hovering outside the library when he came back, rehearsing what she intended to say. Perhaps it would be wiser if she just packed her bags and went back to England, she thought uneasily. She wasn't doing much good here, and the situation disturbed her.

And not just the situation, she admitted honestly as Alex walked back along the corridor towards her. Virginia's husband disturbed her, not least because he was her friend's husband and she was attracted to him. It was crazy, she knew, particularly in the present circumstances. But the awareness she felt just wouldn't go away, and she couldn't stay here and let it develop.

However, Alex had ideas of his own, and when she started to say that if he didn't mind she'd say goodnight too, he shook his head. 'Join me in a nightcap before you retire,' he drawled, moving towards her so that to avoid him she was obliged to back into the library. 'What'll it be? White wine again? Or will you share my choice? Scotch?'

'Don't you think——?'

The words were out before she could prevent them, and Alex's mouth took on a mocking twist. 'Don't I think—what?' he enquired, following her into the library and closing the heavy doors behind him. 'You have an annoying tendency of starting sentences and not finishing them, Miss Richards. For instance, I still don't know what you were going to say when you started telling us about your particular field of litigation.'

Camilla swallowed. She had thought he had forgotten that, and it was disconcerting to find he hadn't. It was equally disconcerting to realise that his mind had not been blunted by the amount of wine he had consumed, and she had to make a determined effort to counter his cool-eyed appraisal.

'So,' he said, walking across to the tray of drinks that resided on an inlaid cabinet, 'talk to me.'

'Wh...what about?'

Camilla feigned ignorance, and his mouth compressed. 'OK. Let's start with what you'd like to drink. And don't say nothing. I hate drinking alone.'

Camilla sighed. 'Do...do you have any mineral water?'

Alex gave her a dry look. 'Water?'

'Or fruit juice. Anything will do.'

'But not Scotch?'

'I...don't like whisky,' she replied quickly. 'I don't like any spirits, really. Just...just...'

'Wine,' he said flatly, finishing the sentence for her. 'All right. Here you are. Try that.'

He held out a stemmed wine glass to her, and Camilla took it reluctantly. But she was so anxious about what it was he was giving her that she didn't pay enough attention to the actual exchange of the glass. In consequence, her fingers brushed his, and in an effort to avoid them she almost dropped it.

The incident brought both his hands to save it, and for a moment one of them was wrapped around hers. She felt the cool hardness of his skin against hers, the strength behind the long brown fingers that trapped hers so easily within their grasp, and her throat contracted. He was so close; much closer than he had been all evening and, against her will, she inhaled the warm heat of his body. He smelled so clean and fresh and masculine, with only the faintest hint of musk to indicate that he, too, was affected by their increased awareness of one another. She looked up at him almost instinctively, and eyes as dark as sable swept over her startled face. But they were not sympathetic eyes. They were narrowed and enigmatic, staring at her from between thick lashes, and no emotion entered their depths as he released her.

Trying to still her leaping senses, Camilla looked down into her glass as Alex poured his own drink. She tried to concentrate on wondering what it was he had given her, but the actual content of the drink was of infinitely less importance than what was happening to her here. Dear God, she thought, she had never experienced such a feeling of sexuality; never been aware of her own body as a counterpart to any man's before. Sex, as she defined it, was a delineation of the genes, an acknowledgement of the body's physical needs, a necessary part of procreation. Her own experiences had not led her to believe it could be any more than that, certainly not this sudden loss of control in which her own identity was in grave danger of being obliterated.

'So...' Alex had poured himself a generous measure of Scotch and come back to her '...you were about to tell me what you were going to say before supper. What is it you don't deal in, Miss Richards?'

She swallowed. 'Please—must we be so...so formal? As your mother said, my name's Camilla——'

'I know what your name is,' he retorted, swallowing a mouthful of his drink, and surveying her with impatient eyes. 'Answer my question, why don't you?' He paused. 'Or can't you?'

Camilla wished he would go and sit down. She wished that she could sit down, but, short of taking the initiative and doing so, she was obliged to stay where she was.

'I...I can't remember what the question was!' she exclaimed, playing for time, and his lean face darkened ominously.

'Yes, you can,' he contradicted coldly. 'I want to know what it is you don't deal in, and I'd advise you to stop playing games. It's late, and I'm in no mood to be made a fool of.'

'I'm not making a fool of you.' Camilla sipped her drink almost unthinkingly, and broke into a spontaneous cough. 'Ugh, what is this? I asked for fruit juice.'

Alex's mouth compressed. 'It is fruit juice,' he told her grimly. 'With ice, and a touch of tequila. It won't hurt you.' His tone became sardonic. 'I promise.'

Camilla viewed the drink with definite misgivings. 'Even so——'

'Oh, for God's sake...!'

Alex glared at her, and although she knew she should stick to her guns Camilla gave in. 'All right,' she said, and as if to prove she meant it she took another sip from the glass. 'I suppose it's very nice.'

'Your approval overwhelms me,' he said acidly. 'Shall we continue?'

This time Camilla didn't make the mistake of trying to avoid the question. Instead, she hesitated only a moment before saying, 'I...don't deal in...lots of things. But——' this, as he looked as if he was about to break in again '—I think the one you mean is—*was*—divorce.'

Alex regarded her closely. 'Virginia mentioned divorce to you?' he queried tensely, and Camilla closed her eyes for a second before continuing.

'No,' she said, speaking fearlessly for the first time. 'No, she didn't——'

'Then why did you——?'

'Oh—it was the tone of her letter,' she admitted unwillingly. 'I...I sort of got the impression that...that she wasn't...happy.'

'Happy!' Alex stared at her. 'You got the impression that she wasn't happy? That's not what you said before.'

'No.'

'Then why did you come here?'

'I told you. Virginia invited me.'

'Invited you? Or asked for your professional assistance?'

'Invited me.' Camilla was indignant. 'Oh...I admit I was worried about her. But she knew there was nothing I could do here. Not...not professionally, anyway.'

Alex studied her for several heart-stopping moments, and then, as if accepting what she had said, he turned away, emptying his glass as he did so. There was nothing unusual in the action. Indeed, in other circumstances Camilla would scarcely have paid any attention to such an ordinary procedure, but Alex's attitude was one of weary acquiescence, and her heart overrode her common sense. Instead of putting down her drink and making good her escape while she had the chance, she stayed where she was, the need to do—or say—something to comfort him overwhelming all other considerations.

'I...I'm sure there's no need to worry,' she burst out recklessly. 'Virginia may have just needed to get away for a while, to be on her own—with her daughter, of course,' she added hastily. 'You...you probably had . . . had an argument or something. This . . . this may be her way to attract your attention——'

'My attention!' Alex turned back on her then, his dark face suffused with anger. 'My God! Do you think that's all this is? A lover's quarrel? A family argument that ended in Virginia's walking out?' He uttered a harsh laugh, and as if growing impatient with the empty glass in his hands he threw it at the bookshelves, where it shattered into a thousand pieces. 'God, do you think I'd be going to all this trouble if I thought Virginia were in her right mind?'

Camilla backed up against the door. 'Her . . . right . . . mind?' she echoed faintly, a dozen different interpretations splintering in her head. 'You mean . . . you mean . . . Virginia's insane?'

'Sanity?' He glared at her. 'Sanity's a legal term, as you should know only too well. But no, Virginia's not insane; not in the way you mean, anyway. But drugs do bend the mind, don't they? Particularly a mind as receptive to corruption as Virginia's!'

CHAPTER SIX

IN SPITE of waking with a nasty taste in her mouth the next morning, Camilla had slept soundly. Which was something of a miracle, she thought, considering the state she had been in when she had reached her room the night before. Indeed, she had been sure she wouldn't sleep a wink, but the tequila must have been stronger than she'd thought. Alex's 'touch' must have been fairly heavy, she suspected. But it was probably just as well, in the circumstances.

Cleaning her teeth in the bathroom, she felt the full horror of what he had told her sweep over her once again. Virginia was an addict, addicted to so-called 'hard' drugs, like heroin and cocaine. She had been in and out of clinics for the past three years, but she had been taking drugs for much, much longer than that.

Which meant she must have been using drugs before she got married, Camilla acknowledged now, straightening to view her pale complexion without enthusiasm. If what Alex said was true, Virginia had started smoking marijuana as soon as she had left school. In the circles she had moved in it was considered no more addictive than ordinary cigarettes or alcohol. And it was freely available, as Camilla knew from her own experience.

Not that Camilla had ever felt the urge to experiment with drugs. Her experience had come from the contacts she made in the course of her work, contacts that had swiftly persuaded her that any kind of drug abuse was dangerous. She had learned that the need for the stimulant soon outweighed all else, and often homes, and families, were sacrificed to finance the habit.

And that was what Virginia had done—*was doing*. Again, if Alex was telling the truth Virginia would do anything to satisfy her craving. Even to the extent of kidnapping her own daughter in an effort to force Alex to give her what she wanted, Camilla acknowledged grimly.

But what did she want? Camilla could only guess. The letter she had received had spoken of cruelty and abuse— but who was abusing whom? And, again according to Alex, it wasn't the first time Virginia had put her daughter's life in jeopardy. Once before she had used the child as a blind to reach a dealer in Honolulu. And, on top of the horror of taking her own daughter into such places, she had crashed the car on the way back. Virginia hadn't been hurt. Predictably, all she had received were a few cuts and bruises. But Maria had suffered a fractured skull, and for days she had been unconscious.

Oh, Virginia had been contrite, Alex had told Camilla bitterly. While Maria lay in a hospital bed, she had been full of remorse, even agreeing that she couldn't go on destroying herself and putting a child's life in danger. So another stint at a rehabilitation centre had followed, reinforcing, he had hoped, her tenuous conviction that there was no future in continuing the habit.

But recently the situation had begun to deteriorate once more. And, although Virginia had denied using any of the substances she had used in the past, the signs were unmistakable.

However, even Alex had not expected Virginia to involve Maria again. After what had happened before he had believed she had learned her lesson, and, although she had shown no great affection for the child in the past, he had never dreamed she might deliberately take Maria away. When he had left for New York ten days ago he had warned his staff to be on the alert, but that was all. And when Virginia had said she wanted to go shopping in Honolulu, no one had thought anything of it. Ever since the accident Carlo or one of the security guards always chauffeured her into town, and when she and Maria had been dropped at the Ala Moana centre it was on the understanding that they would be picked up again a couple of hours later.

It was only when Virginia and Maria hadn't shown up at the appointed time that suspicions were aroused. And even then no one had wanted to worry Alex unnecessarily. In consequence, it had been a full twenty-four hours before they had caught up with him in New York and, by then, it was too late. Virginia had left the island under an assumed name, and the trail was already going cold.

Now Camilla used her damp hands to push her hair back from her face, and stared unblinkingly at her reflection. Was it true? she wondered. Could Virginia have done all the things her husband accused her of? But, if she hadn't, where was she? And what was she doing?

Camilla sighed. She didn't have any answers. And, although she didn't like to condemn her friend unheard, she couldn't help remembering how Virginia had looked the last time she'd seen her. The edginess, the lack of concentration, the brittle exuberance which Camilla had excused as nerves. Was it possible that, even then, Virginia had been on the point of breaking?

Leaving the bathroom, Camilla padded into the bedroom, where coffee was cooling on the bedside table. Mama Lu must have brought it earlier, while she was still asleep, and decided not to wake her. Or *had* that been Mama Lu's decision? Camilla pondered. Perhaps her host had regretted his outburst of the night before, and was eager to avoid another encounter. For he must know she would have questions, even if last night she had been too stunned to make any coherent response.

Seating herself on the edge of the bed, Camilla poured herself a cup of coffee, and sipped it slowly. Her mind was in a turmoil, and she didn't know what she was going to do. The simplest thing would be to book herself a return flight to London, and leave Virginia and Alex to seal their own fate. It was nothing to do with her, really. Now that she had some inkling of what had been going on it would be much more sensible to go home.

And less embarrassing, she acknowledged ruefully. Even if Virginia did come back, she would be the last person her friend would want to see. Whatever reasons Virginia had had for writing had been negated by her actions. She wasn't a prisoner here; she hadn't been mistreated. And, if what Alex had told her was true, she shouldn't believe a word Virginia had said.

There was another reason why she should leave too, Camilla admitted now, putting the empty cup back on the tray. Aside from everything else, she had her own feelings to consider. It would probably be extremely unwise to stay here while Alex was going through such a difficult time. Actions could be misconstrued, and when emotions were near the surface all sorts of mistakes could be made.

For example, the way she had reacted to him the night before, she reminded herself unwillingly. In ordinary circumstances she would never have felt that way about ánother woman's husband, never let him know she was aware of him in such a shameless way. For he had been aware of it, she conceded, which was probably why he'd told her what he had. She had the feeling that baring his soul to a virtual stranger was something Alex Conti had never done before. It had just been his way of defusing a potentially embarrassing situation; of reminding her why she was here.

And that was probably why she had been left to sleep on this morning, she thought with a sigh. Alex would obviously prefer to prolong the interval till he had to speak to her again. He might even wish he didn't have to speak to her at all. After all, he had enough problems to contend with, without shouldering any more.

Still not sure what she was going to do, Camilla took a shower and dressed, trying not to think about anything. Beyond her windows, another perfect morning was unfolding, and as she dried her hair, and threaded it into a chunky pigtail, she let the beauty of the view console her. If nothing else she had seen Hawaii, she thought wistfully, or at least a small part of it. It was a pity she hadn't been able to enjoy it, but she would have some memories to take back to England with her.

She had no problem finding her way outside this morning. The sun-splashed terrace was just as delightful as on the previous day, and although it was after nine o'clock the table was waiting, but laid for one—as she had expected.

She didn't immediately go and sit down. Instead, she walked to the edge of the area and looked down on to the beach. The palms that grew in such profusion at the edge of the sand were dark against a sky as blue as periwinkles, and along the shoreline a clump of seaweed had been washed up by the tide. It was the cause of some dispute between a pair of squabbling sea-birds, and their raucous cries rose shrilly over the murmur of the tide.

She was so intent on watching the quarrelling gulls that she didn't hear the sound of footsteps behind her, and she jumped almost guiltily when a voice said, 'Good morning.'

It was Alex, and Camilla's confusion was compounded by the fact that he was the last person she had expected to see. He was supposed to have had his breakfast and left for his office in Honolulu, she thought dizzily. Instead of which he was standing there, lean and dark and masculine, in black trousers and a white shirt, regarding her as if he had nothing more than her well-being on his mind.

'Um . . . good morning,' she responded at last, putting her hands behind her and bracing herself against the low wall of the terrace. However, the unconscious provocation of the action exposed the rounded swell of her small breasts, and as realisation dawned she felt a corresponding awareness harden her nipples. The taut peaks pushed against the thin fabric of her shirt—hopelessly noticeable, she thought frustratedly—and she straightened abruptly and folded her arms.

If Alex noticed this ludicrous display he gave no sign of it, and she was grateful. God, she thought impatiently, she was acting like an adolescent!

'How are you?' he asked now, and she made a conscious effort to act casually.

'Fine,' she said, forcing a smile to relax the muscles of her face. 'But . . . I'm afraid I overslept again.'

'It happens.' Alex's lean features were politely composed. 'I guess it's the jet lag. It can be that way sometimes. Though, in my experience, it's harder flying east than west. At least this way you gain some time, instead of losing it.'

Camilla nodded. 'Oh, yes.' Then, feeling compelled to say something about Virginia, she added, 'I suppose there's no . . .'

Her voice trailed away, but Alex clearly knew what she had been going to ask. 'No,' he said heavily, and to her relief he turned away. 'No word,' he appended, trailing his fingers along the crisp white cloth that covered the table. 'It's as if they've disappeared off the face of the earth.'

Camilla moistened her lips. 'Your investigator——'

'Has found nothing. Not a trace. Since they hired a car in Los Angeles, and drove south to San Diego, there have been no sightings whatsoever. And, believe me, there've been plenty of people looking.'

Camilla sighed. 'I'm sorry.'

'You're sorry?' He turned then, a frown drawing his darkly defined brows together. 'Why should you be sorry? It's not your fault, is it?'

'Well, of course not, but——'

'But—what?' He gave her a narrow-eyed appraisal. 'If, as you say, you haven't seen Virginia for six years, why the hell should you be sorry?'

Camilla stiffened. 'Don't you believe me?'

'Yes, if you say so.' But his response was grudging, to say the least, and Camilla laced her fingers together.

'Well, it's the truth,' she said tightly, realising it was much harder to argue a point in shorts and a T-shirt than it was in a business suit. 'And I have no idea why she wrote to me after all this time. Not . . . not if she intended not to be here.'

Alex was regarding her intently now. 'You're sure about that?'

'Of course.' Camilla was indignant. 'I hope you don't think I insisted on coming. It wasn't my idea at all. I . . . I had other plans.'

Alex frowned. 'Other plans?'

'It is the summer season,' she reminded him shortly. 'I . . . was going on holiday with . . . with a friend. I had to cancel that when I decided to come here.'

'Ah.' Alex pushed his fingers into the low waistband of his trousers, resting on his hips at the back. He considered for a moment, and then said flatly, 'A male friend.'

'What?'

Camilla was briefly bewildered, and he explained. 'The friend you were going on holiday with,' he prompted. 'You don't wear a ring, so I assume you're not married.'

Camilla caught her breath. For a moment she couldn't speak. She had never imagined he might have noticed anything about her, least of all whether or not she was wearing a wedding-ring.

But, as if he was growing impatient with her wide-eyed consternation, Alex's hands fell to his sides and he made a careless gesture. 'It doesn't matter,' he said. 'I shouldn't have asked. It's nothing to do with me.' He glanced over his shoulder towards the house. 'You must be hungry. I'll get Lee to fetch you some coffee, and you can tell him what you'd like to eat.'

Camilla took an involuntary step towards him. 'It...it was a woman, actually,' she said, compelled to correct his assumption. 'We were going pony-trekking in Wales. She still is, as it happens. We were going with a group, so one more or less doesn't matter.'

'I see.'

But Alex didn't seem interested any longer, and Camilla guessed that once again he was only being polite. And, as if on cue, Wong Lee chose that moment to come out of the house, successfully curtailing any chance she might have had of prolonging their conversation.

Not that she could be angry with the cheery-faced Chinese man. His manner was so unfailingly polite, and his eager efforts to persuade her that rolls and coffee did not constitute a proper breakfast were almost comical. She was sufficiently diverted not to notice when Alex left them, and it was not until the little man had departed to inform Mama Lu of her decision that she realised she was alone.

In the event, she accepted one of Mama Lu's blueberry muffins, tucked into the basket of warm croissants the housekeeper brought her. And that, combined with several more cups of the deliciously aromatic beverage, which bore no resemblance to the coffee she made for herself at home, was all she wanted. It wasn't just the conversation with Alex that had disconcerted her. She simply wasn't very hungry. Now that she was alone again her worries about Virginia had re-surfaced, and she wondered how any mother could do to her daughter what Virginia was doing. If she had just taken the child as a blind, as she had done before, why hadn't she sent her home again before she left the island? Surely, wherever she was, the little girl could only be a nuisance to her? Unless she had some other motive for taking her, a motive they had yet to find out...

She was pondering this equation when a shadow fell across the table. Expecting it to be either Wong Lee, or Mama Lu, come to chivvy her about the poor breakfast she had made, Camilla looked up with a rueful smile, a smile that faltered unmistakably when she encountered Alex's dark stare.

However, his expression was not condemnatory. On the contrary, there was a certain detachment in his gaze, and his tone was distant as he said, 'I have to leave now. Much as I might deplore the fact, I have a business to run, and at least it keeps my mind occupied.' He paused. 'But I was wondering if you'd had any further thoughts about what you're going to do.'

'What I'm going to do?' Camilla blinked. 'But I thought I——'

'I know what you said yesterday,' he interrupted her abruptly, 'but it seems fairly obvious that Virginia's not going to get in touch with you.'

'Does it?'

'Well, doesn't it?' He took a deep breath. 'You've been here more than twenty-four hours—nearly forty-eight hours, actually—and, unless you know something that I don't, there's been no contact. Has there?'

'Well...no...'

'So, tell me about it. Do you really think Virginia is going to risk my finding out where she is by phoning you?'

'Perhaps not.' Camilla felt cold. 'In other words, you want me to leave.'

Alex raked the fingers of one hand through his hair, bringing the hand to rest at the back of his neck. Then, tipping his head back against the obstruction, he uttered a weary sound.

'I think it would be best,' he said at last, bringing his head forward again to look at her. 'Don't you?'

Camilla tore her gaze away, and looked down at the table. 'I...perhaps.' She lifted her shoulders in a helpless gesture. 'I don't know if I'll be able to get a flight today, though——'

'You don't have to leave *today*,' retorted Alex impatiently. 'I'm not that unreasonable. In fact...' He broke off, and then, levelling his tone, he added, 'Why don't you book into one of the hotels on Waikiki for a few days? I could get my secretary to arrange it. At my expense, of course.'

'No!' Camilla's reply was instantaneous, and the look she momentarily cast up at him left him in no doubt as to her response to his offer. 'No, I...I'll phone the airline this morning. If you have no objections, of course. Otherwise, I suppose I could take a taxi into town——'

'Don't be stupid!' Alex's reaction to this was as aggressive as hers had been. 'You don't have to phone the airline. I'll make any enquiries that are necessary myself.'

'I'd really rather——'

'I've said I'll do it,' he told her harshly, turning away. 'In any case, it's too late to do anything about it today. The morning flight has already left, and the afternoon plane to Los Angeles is usually over-subscribed. As I say, leave it with me, and I'll let you know what I've arranged.'

Camilla shrugged. 'If you insist.'

'I do.'

But Alex seemed restless, and although he had said he was leaving he was making no move to do so. On the contrary, he seemed mesmerised by the view Camilla had been looking at earlier, and the silence stretched between them, fairly simmering with tension.

However, Camilla was the guest here, and, deciding she was being ungracious, she made an effort to recover her sense of balance. After all, he was just being polite, she told herself. Even if his kindness smacked of *noblesse oblige*.

'I...I did wonder,' she said, annoyed to find her voice wasn't entirely steady. 'I did wonder if...if you had considered that Virginia might have had some other reason for...for taking Maria with her. I mean,' she hastened on, as his brooding gaze was turned again in her direction, 'it's possible that she had a reason——'

'She does.' His reply was savage. 'It's her way of making sure I do what she wants.'

'Well, yes. I can see that.' Camilla didn't exactly know what she did see, and she had the feeling that Alex wasn't interested in her theories anyway. Nevertheless, she went on, 'But you think her running away has to do with...with her addiction——'

'It does.'

'But what if it was something else?'

'Something else?' She had his attention now, though she doubted he was really listening to her. 'What else could there be?'

Camilla swallowed. 'Well...a divorce?'

'A divorce?' Alex's expression was pitying now. 'You're not serious!'

'Why not?'

'Why not? I'll tell you why not!' Alex was scathing. 'Because Virginia knows she can have a divorce any time she cares to ask for one.'

'Does she?'

Camilla's response was barely audible, and Alex's mouth twisted with some emotion she couldn't identify. 'Yes,' he said now. 'Yes, she can have a divorce. God, Camilla, what kind of a life do you think we have together? Do you have some romantic idea that love can survive the kind of marriage we've had? How many times can someone lie to you, before you realise they're never going to tell the truth? That it's a foreign language to them? Virginia and I passed the point of no return years ago, but I, gullible fool that I was, still felt some responsibility for her.'

In spite of the heat of the day, Camilla shivered. 'I...I didn't know.'

'No.' His answer was an acceptance of her ignorance. 'No, I guess you didn't. Or you wouldn't have come here, right?'

'Right.' Camilla pressed her hands down on the table and stood up. 'I...thank you for telling me.'

'God, don't thank me!' Alex made a sound of frustration. 'I probably shouldn't have laid this on you. It's not your concern, and it isn't fair to expect you to make a judgement, either way.' He closed his eyes for a moment against the images only he could see, 'I must be getting maudlin. I'm not in the habit of unburdening myself to anyone.'

Camilla shook her head. 'Sometimes it helps,' she murmured, not quite knowing what to say, and Alex grimaced.

'Oh, yes. I guess you're used to listening while strangers pour out their troubles, aren't you? It's part of your job. Well, they say confession's good for the soul, don't they?'

Camilla sighed. 'I...don't consider you a...a stranger,' she amended carefully. 'And...this isn't part of my job.'

'Isn't it?'

He was looking directly at her now, and Camilla moved round her chair to grip the back with nervous fingers. 'No.'

'No.' His eyes widened, the pupils expanding to fill the iris so that they looked almost black. 'You're a good friend, aren't you, Camilla?' he added, his tone vaguely self-derisive. 'You wouldn't dream of lying to me, would you?'

Camilla didn't know how to answer that. For some reason the atmosphere between them was suddenly taut with unspoken emotions, and a trickle of moisture ran chillingly down her spine. He was staring at her as if he could see right through her shallow façade of composure, into the forbidden tangle of her thoughts. And the knowledge caused her heart to quicken, and the blood to race like liquid fire through her veins. Dear God, he couldn't know what she was thinking, could he? He couldn't know how much she wanted to console him; to comfort him; to touch him——

'I have to go.'

His words were abrupt and decisive, severing the humid air with the incisiveness of a knife. Whatever thoughts he had had, he was not prepared to discuss them, and Camilla hung on to the back of the chair as he pulled his car keys out of his pocket, and tossed them in his hand.

'You'll be all right?'

Camilla wondered what he would say if she said no, but discretion was the better part of valour, and she nodded. 'Of course.'

Alex frowned suddenly. 'I could get someone to give you a quick tour of the island,' he offered, and she sensed he was feeling guilty for some reason. Or was it just her imagination working overtime once again? 'I guess you'd like to see some of the parks and gardens. And there's Pearl Harbor, of course. Everyone wants to see that.'

'No.' She tempered her refusal with a tight smile. 'I...don't need entertaining. Besides,' she gestured towards the beach, 'I can always swim, can't I? And sunbathe, too, if I want.'

'So long as you don't get burned,' agreed Alex warningly, and then, realising he was getting heavy again, he added, 'But, if you change your mind about that tour, ring me. I know Grant would be only too happy to spend the day with a beautiful woman.' He paused, and pulled a wry face. 'Oh, I forgot. You don't know Grant, do you? Well, he's my——'

'Cousin,' put in Camilla unthinkingly. 'I know.' And, as Alex's eyes narrowed, she felt the colour invade her cheeks once again. 'We...we've met.'

'You have?' Alex was polite, but she could feel the hostility that had entered his eyes at her words. 'How interesting. D'you want to tell me when?'

Camilla sighed. 'Yesterday, of course. I assumed he'd have told you.' She shifted a little defensively. 'Didn't Mama Lu say anything?'

'No. No, she didn't.' Alex's mouth thinned. 'But then, I guess we've all had other things on our minds, haven't we?' He clenched the car keys in his balled fist. 'So—he came here? What did he want?'

Camilla felt a rising sense of indignation overtaking her other emotions. He was acting as if she had somehow betrayed his trust, when, in fact, she would have much preferred not to have met his cousin.

'I don't know,' she said now, and there was an edge of impatience to her voice. 'Why don't you ask him?'

'Oh, I will.' Alex's eyes were cold. 'Depend on it.'

Anger swamped her. Just because she had admitted that Grant Blaisdell had come here in his absence he had reverted to treating her as if she was a suspect in the case. My God, the man was paranoid! She'd hardly have told him she had met Grant if she had anything to hide, would she?

With an audible sound of defeat, she let go of the chair and started across the terrace. To hell with him, she thought crossly. He could deal with it in his own way, but she didn't have to be part of it. If he wanted to speak to her again he could bloody well ask to do so. She'd be damned if she was going to stay here and bear the brunt of his frustration.

She hadn't expected he would come after her, but he did, and she had barely reached the foot of the spiral staircase when his hand descended on her shoulder. 'Wait,' he said harshly, and, although wisdom dictated that she ignore him and go on, the weight of his restraining fingers was a strong deterrent. Besides, she was intensely conscious of the spreading heat that had invaded her stomach when he had touched her, and she wasn't entirely sure her legs would carry her up the steps.

Still, she had to do something to retain her sanity, and, tipping her head towards him, she adopted her most intimidating court-room stare. 'Well?'

Alex met her gaze without flinching. Instead, his eyes held hers with a steady appraisal that accelerated her already racing heart and caused a corresponding quickening of her breathing. The world seemed to shrink to embrace just the two of them, with the hard pressure of his flesh against hers as its core.

And, as if he, too, was aware of the sexual energy flowing between them, his fingers softened, gentled, his thumb moving down over the narrow bone of her clavicle with almost involuntary possession. She caught her breath as his thumb invaded the neckline of her shirt to brush against her leaping pulse, that beat in the hollow at the base of her throat, and her tongue parted her lips when his gaze dropped to her mouth.

'I'm sorry,' he said huskily, and for a minute she hadn't the faintest idea what he was talking about.

'Are you?' she got out breathily, and, unconsciously, she leaned towards him. His lean mouth was only inches from hers, and she ached to feel it moving against hers, to have his tongue invading her mouth...

'Yes,' he replied, but now the husky note had hardened to a harsh denial, and as he stepped back his hand fell away. 'I guess we all make mistakes,' he added and, brushing past her, he took the stairs two at a time.

CHAPTER SEVEN

THE enquiries Camilla made were not encouraging. The airline office in Honolulu assured her they would do their best to accommodate her, but they already had a stand-by list for both today and tomorrow. However, they were sure they'd be able to get her on a flight to Los Angeles after the weekend, and they took her telephone number, just in case they had a spate of cancellations.

Not that Camilla held out much hope. As Alex had said, it was the busiest time of the year, and, although the islands didn't really have a season as such, most people took their holidays through the recognised summer months. In consequence, she was obliged to stay here for at least another two days, and the prospect was not appealing.

Of course, Alex had said he would make her travel arrangements for her, but after what had happened that morning Camilla was desperate to do something to help herself. She wanted to get away before she had to meet Alex again if possible. She had made an absolute fool of herself earlier, and the thought of facing him again made her cringe with embarrassment.

It was useless to tell herself that, in fact, she had done nothing, that she hadn't grabbed him physically and forced him to suffer her *mauling*. She knew that was too strong a word to use to describe what had actually happened, but it made her feel better to think of it in those terms. If she could justify her unsubtle come-on as the involuntary counterpart to his treatment of her perhaps she could live with herself. Otherwise, she had humiliated herself totally and utterly.

Yet she had nothing to blame herself for, she argued defensively as she squatted on the sand later that morning. After making her call to the airline office she had gone along to her room and changed into fresh shorts and a bikini. She knew Alex wouldn't be back until late that afternoon, and she had decided to take a dip in the ocean. It probably wasn't the right thing to do, with Virginia and Maria still missing, and her own relationship with Virginia's husband in such a state of turmoil, but she was hot and sticky, and she needed to cool down.

She could have taken another shower, of course. That would probably have been the sympathetic thing to do; but she didn't. The ocean was just lying there, waiting to be enjoyed, and she couldn't fly all this way without taking a dip in the Pacific.

Nevertheless, fifteen minutes after going down to the beach Camilla was still sitting with her knees drawn up to make a support for her chin. The sun was hot on her shoulders, and in spite of the breeze she could feel its heat probing her flesh. She was probably going to get burned, she thought resignedly, but she made no attempt to cover herself with the towel she had brought with her. It would probably serve her right, she decided. And at least it was burning away the lingering imprint of Alex's fingers.

She sighed. Maybe he hadn't noticed, she consoled herself, not altogether convincingly. After all, he had been the one who had initiated the contact. Maybe his reaction had been a response to his own reckless behaviour. He might not have realised that she had been involved.

But she had leaned towards him, she reminded herself depressingly. She had allowed her tongue to appear, and gazed up at him like some lovesick fool. No, *sex-hungry* fool, she corrected herself bitterly. Oh, God! He probably thought she was desperate for a man! She'd already told him she had been going on holiday with another woman. Made a point of it, in fact, she remembered miserably. Perhaps she should do as he suggested and find herself an hotel room until she could get a flight out of here. There was bound to be some hotel on Waikiki with a single room available. When she went back to the house she should make a few calls. It was the next best thing to leaving the island.

Her shoulders were beginning to prickle with the heat, and, deciding there was no point in crucifying her flesh any longer, she stood up and kicked off her canvas boots. Then, unfastening the button of her shorts, she dropped them to her ankles. It was the first time she had worn a bikini this year, and as well as noticing how pale she looked Camilla was intensely conscious of the windows of the house behind her. Not that she really thought anyone might be watching her. But Grant Blaisdell had arrived uninvited before and, remembering that he hadn't told Alex about his visit, she couldn't altogether rule out his intervention.

But no one watched from the balcony as she ran into the ocean, and Camilla was relieved. And it was heaven to feel the silky water lapping about her. The initial feeling as she plunged into the waves was one of chill, but it didn't last. The temperature of the water had to be at least seventy degrees, she decided, and its sparkling salty tang was both soothing and exhilarating.

The beach shelved fairly quickly, and there were waving gardens of seaweed beneath her kicking legs. The tide was also fairly strong, and until she got beyond the point where the surf broke its roll she kept finding herself engulfed by the creaming swell. In consequence, she was forced to go out further than she had intended, and although she was a good swimmer she didn't stay out long.

Nevertheless, she did enjoy it, and by the time she reached her depth again and waded up on to the sand she was feeling infinitely brighter. She had been over-reacting, she decided, picking up her towel and drying her face. In a couple of days she'd be out of here, out of Alex's life forever. And Virginia's, she reminded herself uneasily. In heaven's name, where was she?

She was standing with her towel about her bare shoulders, gazing unseeingly at the ocean, when she heard someone calling her name. 'Miss Richards! *Camilla!* You wanna come and take a call?'

A call? For her? Camilla blinked, and looked round to see Mama Lu standing, waving her arms about, at the top of the terrace steps. The housekeeper was evidently trying to attract her attention, and without

stopping to put on her clothes Camilla picked up her
shorts and boots and started towards her.

But her mind was buzzing. Who could be calling her?
she wondered. Who knew she was here, apart from Grant
Blaisdell and the Contis? She determinedly refused to
consider that it could be Virginia, even though the idea
refused to be dislodged. Mama Lu would have recognised Virginia's voice, she told herself impatiently. Better
than she would, probably.

And then she remembered the call she had made to
the airline office. Of course, it would be the girl there
returning her call. Maybe she had found her a cancellation for today after all. No matter how empty that
made her feel, she had to take it.

Mama Lu was waiting impatiently, and Camilla kept
her voice free of expression with an effort. 'Who... who
is it?' she asked, conscious of the brevity of the bikini,
which seemed so unsuitable in the circumstances. But
she had put it in as an afterthought, never dreaming what
she was going to find at Kumaru.

'She says she's calling from the New Zealand Airlines
office,' declared the housekeeper, accompanying Camilla
into the house. 'You can take it here.' She indicated the
phone in the garden-room, a delicate green instrument
that was virtually invisible against a bank of orchids.
'Just pick it up.'

Camilla blinked again. *New Zealand Airlines!* she was
thinking blankly. She hadn't flown with New Zealand
Airlines; she certainly hadn't called New Zealand
Airlines. Unless... She frowned. It was possible that
the airline she had called had tried to fix her up with an
alternative. She hadn't realised there was such a rapport
between them.

'Thank you,' she called, as Mama Lu hauled her bulk
up the curving staircase, and the housekeeper lifted one
hand in silent acknowledgement. Then, putting the receiver to her ear, she said, 'This is Camilla Richards.'

'Miss Richards?' The voice was vaguely Chinese in
intonation, the words clipped and lisping.

'Yes.' As Camilla confirmed her identity she heard
the distinctive click as the upstairs phone was discon-

nected. Evidently Mama Lu had replaced her receiver, and she waited impatiently for the girl to continue.

Then, *'Camilla?'* she heard in a hushed whisper. 'Camilla, it's me: Virginia.'

'Virginia!' Camilla's mouth went dry, and she sank down on to the cushions of a basket chair nearby. 'Virginia, for heaven's sake! Where are you?'

'Never mind that now.' Virginia spoke urgently, her voice gaining in volume as she continued. 'You don't think that old fool recognised my voice, do you? What did she say? Did she tell you it was the airline?'

Camilla swallowed. 'She...she said it was New Zealand Airlines, yes.'

'Well, that was all right, wasn't it?'

'I suppose...' Camilla shook her head. 'But I didn't fly with New Zealand Airlines.'

'Didn't you? Damn! I was sure you would.' Virginia sounded frustrated. 'Oh, well, never mind. You'll have to make some excuse as to why they would be calling you. It was the only thing I could think of.'

'But why? Why did you have to disguise your voice in the first place?'

'Are you kidding?' Virginia snorted. 'You've been there three days, and you don't know that yet?'

Camilla sighed. 'Virginia,' she said the name again, and then, realising how exposed she was in the garden-room with its open doors and spiral staircase, she lowered her voice, 'what's going on? What are you doing? Why did you walk out when you knew I was coming?'

'I didn't know.' Virginia expelled her breath noisily. 'Or, at least, I couldn't be sure. In any case, that's not important now. I want to know what Alex is doing. Is he still looking for me in San Diego?'

'I imagine so.' Camilla caught her breath. 'Is that where you are? San Diego? Virginia, you know this is crazy. He's going to find you——'

'Maybe.' Virginia sounded dismissive. 'But I don't want to talk about that now. I didn't make this call to hear what you think. I did what I had to do. That's all you need to know for now.'

Camilla shook her head. 'No, it's not.' She could feel herself getting irritated by the other woman's attitude.

'You got me here under false pretences, Virginia, and I want to know——'

'Not now, Cam. I don't have time to explain my reasons. You're there and that's all that matters. If I need you I'll call.'

'No!'

'What do you mean, no?'

'I mean I'm leaving. Just as soon as I can get a flight. As a matter of fact, I rang the airline this morning.'

'Please don't do that.' Virginia's voice rose perceptibly. 'Not when you've got a ready-made excuse for this call.'

'I'm not going to tell lies, Virginia.'

'But you won't leave. You can't.'

'I have to.'

'Why?' Virginia sounded desperate now. 'For God's sake, Cam, don't do this to me! Is it Alex? What has he been saying about me? Did he ask you to leave? If he's been telling you lies——'

'Virginia——'

'Well, go on. What has he been saying? This isn't all my fault, you know.' Virginia's voice was agitated. 'Look, I can't explain now, but I need you to be there for me.'

'Because of Alex?' Camilla was shocked.

'Yes. No. As I say, I really can't explain now. But everyone tells lies about me. I have no one I can trust. Are you listening, Cam?'

Camilla was listening but she didn't know how to answer. Within a few seconds Virginia had gone from speaking reasonably to shouting down the phone, and Camilla was half afraid to speak in case she said the wrong thing.

'I want to help you, Virginia,' she protested now, choosing her words with care. 'But everyone's worried sick about you and Maria, and I—well, I feel in the way.'

There was an ominous silence, during which Camilla became afraid that Virginia had rung off. But presently she spoke again, and once more she seemed to have herself in control.

'Look,' she said, and, listening to her, Camilla began to suspect what Alex had had to deal with, 'I have my reasons for doing this. I can't tell you what they are. Not yet, anyway. But, if you won't stay for me, stay for Maria.'

'Maria?' Camilla was shocked. 'Virginia, I don't even know Maria. How can my staying here help her? Why... why don't you let her come home? I mean,' she hurried on, 'you may have had your reasons for leaving, as you say, but surely Maria would be...happier...at home.'

'You were going to say *safer*, weren't you?' Virginia exclaimed angrily. 'And you say Alex hasn't poisoned your mind against me! You can't lie to me, Cam. I know you too well. Don't let him turn you against me. I need you.'

'He hasn't. I mean...' once again, Camilla was at a loss for words '...naturally he's worried about you——'

'Not about me,' retorted Virginia. 'Only about Maria. She's all he cares about. Well, I've got her now, and she won't be coming back unless I say so. So he can sweat!'

'Oh, Virginia!' Camilla's hand clenched around the receiver. If only Alex were here, she was thinking desperately, he might know what to say to get through to her.

'Anyway...' with a disturbing lack of consistency, Virginia changed her tone '...what do you think of Alex? Handsome, isn't he? And rich; filthy rich! I certainly landed a live one, wouldn't you say?'

'So why did you leave him? Virginia, I'm sure he cares about you——'

'Stop saying that.' Virginia was scornful. 'I asked you what *you* thought about him. Don't you find him attractive?' She paused. 'Have you tried to console him?'

'*No!*' Camilla was horrified, but she heard Virginia laugh.

'Don't sound so outraged. I know the kind of life you lead in London. All that free sex. I'm sure you've thought about it.'

'I haven't.'

And, in spite of herself, Camilla could feel her anger rekindling. It was all very well telling herself that Virginia was just baiting her, that she wasn't quite *normal*, but her words stung all the same.

'Anyway you're welcome to him,' Virginia went on carelessly. 'I don't want him. Not any more. He hasn't slept with me for God knows how long, and I don't care what he does.'

Camilla couldn't believe what she was hearing, but she had to stop it. 'I...I wouldn't dream of...of...' She couldn't finish. 'Virginia, he's your husband!'

'He doesn't love me,' retorted Virginia harshly. 'I don't think he ever did. I've had to find other ways to amuse myself. Other men. Men who made me feel like a woman, not a——'

'Virginia, stop it!' Camilla's hand was sticking to the receiver, and her whole body felt suffused with heat. 'I—I don't want to talk about your personal affairs. You...you and Alex have to work that out between you.'

'Is that what he said?'

'No.' Camilla's head was beginning to spin with the lack of continuity in the conversation. 'Virginia, please—tell me where you are. At least tell me when you're coming back.'

'I can't.' Virginia sounded almost furtive now. 'I've got to go.'

'Not yet——'

'Why not?'

'Virginia, what am I supposed to do?'

'I've told you: stay.'

'I can't.'

'Why can't you?'

'Because I've told Alex I'm leaving.'

'Tell him you've changed your mind.'

'I can't do that.'

'Why not?'

'Because I can't.' Camilla pressed her lips together. 'Virginia, why are you doing this?'

'Wait and see,' Virginia answered, and Camilla was still digesting that remark when the line went dead.

Fifteen minutes later Camilla stepped out of the shower in her bathroom and wrapped herself in one of the fluffy cream bath-sheets she found stacked on a metal rack.

Then, padding through to the bedroom, she used the end to dry her dripping hair, trying not to consider the problem of what she was going to do now.

Of course, integrity demanded that she tell Alex about the call, and allow him to deal with it. He might even be able to trace its source, though she thought that was only possible while the call was actually connected. The itemised bill she got for her phone at home listed all her out-going calls, and their destination, but not her in-coming ones. Nevertheless, she ought to give him the chance to try.

But how could she? To do so would be to betray Virginia and the friendship they had once had. She put it in the past tense because she couldn't honestly feel that there was any real compatibility between them any longer. However unnatural it might seem, her sympathies were all with Alex, and it was impossible to ignore that.

Even so, the idea of relating the details of her conversation with his wife to Alex was not appealing. Like her letter, Virginia's remarks were not for publication, and she could hardly tell him that she had been asked to stay on like some undercover agent for Virginia.

Which left her only two choices: either she said nothing about the call, and relied on Mama Lu to judge it unworthy of mention; or she lied, as Virginia had asked her to do. Neither one was particularly appealing, but the alternative was equally so.

Wong Lee served her lunch in the cool environs of the dining-room, but Camilla was hardly in a mood to appreciate the shrimps in scooped-out wedges of papaya and served with a spinach salad, or the bananas wrapped in sugary crêpes. It was a pity, she thought, because it was obvious that Mama Lu had gone to some trouble on her account. But food was the furthest thought from her mind, and she was still sitting, staring blindly through the windows, when Alex walked into the dining-room.

Her first instincts were to get to her feet. One look at his grim countenance was enough to warn her that this was no social visit, and she carefully put her fork aside, and clasped her hands together in her lap.

His dark eyes raked her face, and she was glad she wasn't still wearing the skimpy bikini. The button-through blue cheesecloth did have a square neckline, but it wasn't too revealing, and the short skirt was hidden by the hem of the tablecloth. In addition, its cap sleeves hid the pinking flesh on her shoulders, and with her hair drawn back with combs, exposing her pale profile, she was innocence personified. Or so she reassured herself as he came to stand over her.

'Hi.'

His greeting was restrained, and Camilla managed to look up at him quite composedly. 'Hello.'

'You look nice and cool,' he remarked, pulling his tie away from his collar and loosening the top button. 'Did you enjoy your lunch?'

'Oh—yes. It was lovely.' Camilla used one finger to push the plate of crêpes away from her. 'I'm afraid I wasn't very hungry, that's all.'

'No?'

'No.' She moistened her lips. 'I suppose I'm not used to the heat.'

'But Mama Lu tells me you've been swimming,' he countered smoothly. 'Didn't that cool you down?'

Camilla lifted her shoulders. 'A bit.' But she was wondering what else Mama Lu might have told him, and whether, in spite of Virginia's efforts, the housekeeper had recognised her voice. 'The—er—the water was beautiful.'

'How nice.' Alex was watching her closely. 'So...aren't you going to ask me what I'm doing here? Don't you want to know if there's been any news?'

'Has there?' Camilla gazed up at him urgently. Perhaps Virginia had rung him, too. Was it possible that that was what all this was about?

'*God!*' Alex's harsh oath quickly disabused her of that hope. Leaning forward, he rested his knuckles on the table in front of her as he added savagely, 'How do you Englishwomen do it, huh? How do you sit there, looking as if butter wouldn't melt, when all the time you're lying through your teeth? God, it makes me sick!'

'Mr Conti——'

'Don't...' He took a breath and lowered his tone. 'Don't adopt that injured air with me! It won't work. I know. Do you understand me? *I know!* So why don't we cut the garbage and get to basics?'

Camilla abandoned all hope of avoiding a confrontation as she got stiffly to her feet. But she refused to allow him to browbeat her. 'Yes. Why don't we?' she conceded politely. 'If you'd like to tell me what you're talking about, I'll try and give you an answer. What is it you think you know? And what lies am I supposed to have told you? I don't recall——'

'Oh, can it, Camilla, why don't you?' he muttered, pushing himself up from the table and regarding her with weary eyes. 'Virginia's been on the phone to you, hasn't she? Don't bother to answer that. It wasn't a question. She rang you, and told you to stay put, didn't she? Without giving a thought to the fact that I might be monitoring the call.'

'Monitoring the call?' Camilla gulped. 'You mean——?'

'You didn't think I hadn't already considered the fact that she might ring?' Alex demanded scathingly. 'It was on the cards that, sooner or later, she'd try to make contact. She has to want something out of this, doesn't she? Only, when your brains's half scrambled with crack, you don't always think rationally.'

'Oh, God!' Camilla shook her head. 'So Mama Lu didn't——'

'Recognise Virginia's voice? No, I don't think so.'

'Then...how...?'

'All calls to this number are being recorded by the security firm I told you about.'

'Not...the police?'

'Not yet, no.' Alex's mouth was grim. 'I'd prefer to avoid that kind of publicity if I can.'

'I see.'

'Do you?' He regarded her without liking. 'But you were going to lie for her, weren't you? In spite of all I've told you, you're still prepared to give her the benefit of the doubt.'

'No. Yes. Oh, I don't know.' Camilla moved away from the table, and wrapped her hands around the back of her neck. 'I—I didn't know what to do. I was still thinking about it, when...when...'

'When I interrupted you?'

His tone was cynical, and she turned to look at him defensively. 'Yes, as a matter of fact,' she retorted, not caring at that moment whether he believed her or not. 'Virginia's a friend. Whereas you...you——'

'I'm just a stranger, right?' Alex grimaced. 'And what about Maria? Don't you care what happens to her? Or is she just a stranger, too?'

Camilla swallowed. 'Of course I care. And all I did was hesitate about betraying a friend's confidence. You...you don't have to look at me as if I'd committed some terrible crime!'

'How would you like me to look at you?' he countered harshly, and, despite the antagonism between them, the moment was taut with other emotions.

Camilla shook her head. In spite of herself, her eyes were drawn to the lean muscles flexing beneath the thin material of his shirt. The air-conditioning was running, but the cloth was clinging to his skin in places, and the heat of his body reached out to her. Although there were at least a dozen feet between them, she could smell the musky scent of his sweat, and, contrary to what she might have expected, the odour was not offensive to her. Instead, it made her unwillingly aware of the male flesh beneath the formal business suit, and how thin a veneer civilisation really represented.

But then Alex turned away, and she was again left with the uncomfortable awareness of her own complicity. Everyone else was worried sick about Virginia and Maria, and her only contribution was to lust after Virginia's husband. For that was what she was doing: she knew it. But, because something like this had never happened before, she didn't know how to handle it.

'Anyway,' he said, standing with his back to her, gazing out over the balcony and the terrace below, 'it didn't occur to you to warn Mama Lu who was really on the phone, did it? You didn't think that, if I'd known who it was, I might have been able to put a trace on the call?'

Camilla shrugged. 'I . . . I thought things like that had
to be set up beforehand.'

'How do you know they weren't?'

Camilla hesitated. 'Well—I didn't. But . . . but you just
said you hadn't told the police——'

Alex swung round. 'And that's why you didn't do it?'
he demanded contemptuously.

'No. No, you know it wasn't.' Camilla sniffed.
'Did . . . did you have a trace on it?'

'No.' Alex shrugged out of his jacket and tossed it
over one shoulder. 'As you say, I'd need official per-
mission for something like that.'

Camilla bit her lip. 'So . . . so you're no further
forward?'

'I didn't say that.'

She frowned. 'But——'

'Forget it.' His eyes darkened. 'Why should I tell you
anything? We know whose side you're on, don't we?
And it's certainly not mine!'

'That's not true.'

'What's not true?' He crossed the floor then, until he
was standing right in front of her, and she realised that
any faint emotion he might have felt earlier had been
resolutely controlled. 'You take a call from Virginia, and
as far as I know you might never have told me about it.
You sat here, exchanging small talk, when as far as you
were concerned I was still desperate for news of her and
my daughter. And you say you're on *my* side! Stuff it,
Camilla! I don't believe you.'

Camilla quivered. 'I'll go, then.'

'Go?' His eyes narrowed. 'Go where?'

'To . . . to pack my suitcase, of course,' replied Camilla
unevenly. 'It's obvious I can't stay here now——'

'Like hell you can't stay!' Alex's eyes held hers with
savage determination. 'You're not going anywhere,
Camilla. You're staying here. Do you honestly think I'm
going to lose the only lead I've had in nearly two weeks?'

Camilla stepped back. 'You can't expect me to stay
now.'

'Can't I?'

'No.' She moved her hands in a helpless little gesture.
'You . . . you may feel you have some justification for

saying what you did, but you can't force me to remain
in this house. I...I've come to the conclusion it would
be better all round if I went back to England. As...as
soon as Virginia realises I'm not here any more she'll
probably come home. I mean, she's made her point,
hasn't she? She's proved she can do whatever she likes,
and...and my advice to you is that you two should sit
down and talk about this like...like reasonable human
beings——'

'Only Virginia's not a *reasonable* human being,'
snarled Alex angrily. 'For God's sake, what does she
have to do to prove that she's not capable of reasonable
thought? As she said on the phone, she's doing this to
make me sweat. Well, OK, I'm sweating. But is she
coming home? No. And why? Because that's not all she
wants, damn her!'

Camilla was perspiring now. She could feel the line
of sweat beneath her hairline and round the back of her
neck, and no amount of air-conditioning was going to
make it go away. 'But—what *does* she want?' she protested, and Alex closed his eyes against the unknowing
appeal of hers.

'I don't know,' he said through clenched teeth. 'I wish
I did. But until I do you're staying here.'

'Am I?' Camilla held up her head. 'You can't keep
me a prisoner, too.'

'Too?' Alex's eyes opened, and now they were harsh
with warning. 'Don't push me, Camilla. Right now I've
had just about as much as I can take, and I'm in no
mood to be made a fool of a second time. Just remember, you need a passport to get off the island. And
you're going to give me yours, just to avoid any
mistakes.'

CHAPTER EIGHT

CAMILLA was dancing. She was outdoors; on a moonlit terrace; where Chinese lanterns provided a flickering illumination. Music was drifting on the soft evening air, a wonderfully romantic ballad, and the scent of a thousand different blossoms assailed her senses. She was wearing a gorgeous dress; made of silk chiffon, it was a flowing, wraith-like confection, in subtle shades of blue and mauve and grey, that floated about her bare limbs and caught between the legs of her partner. Her hair was loose about her shoulders, a glorious riot of colour, and when she turned her head and it caught the light it turned to fire against her pale skin.

She was excited. She sensed that. Her heart was beating fast, and the blood was thundering through her veins. But it wasn't just the night and the music that was filling her being with such exhilaration. It was the passion she could clearly see in the eyes of the man who was dancing with her. His eyes told her she was radiant; beautiful; *desirable*. And he wanted her...

His arms were around her, and, although they moved to the exotic rhythm of the guitars, it was only an excuse for him to hold her. And he held her so tightly, so close to his lean powerful body, that she could feel every movement he made.

His hands were on her back, her *bare* back, she realised half guiltily. Apart from the flimsy dress, she was wearing nothing else, and the bootlace straps were the only barrier to his touch. The dress dipped to her waist at the back, and his palms were spread against her skin, skin that reacted wildly to his caressing fingers. She arched against him, and he gathered her even closer.

Her own hands were looped behind his head, her fingers threading through the silky darkness of his hair and raking the warm flesh at his nape. When she turned

her head her lips encountered the faintly abrasive skin
of his jawline, and the aroma of his shaving lotion filled
her nostrils. It was a sensual smell, strongly masculine,
like its user, with the hint of bay rum to tantalise her
senses.

Almost instinctively, her tongue slid between her teeth
to touch his skin. She wanted to taste him as well as feel
him, and through that tenuous contact she felt his tight-
ening response. His hands slid down her back to mould
her hips to his, and she felt the hardening pressure of
his arousal against her stomach.

When he bent his head, and his mouth slanted across
hers, she was swept into a dizzying vortex of feeling.
Heat spread from his body into hers, and her blood felt
like liquid fire in her veins. She was suffused with
warmth, and pleasure, and the aching need to wind
herself about this man and never let him go.

His tongue invaded her mouth, hot and wet and pos-
sessive, and a little moan escaped her as he dragged her
even closer. His tongue wound about hers, sucking it
into his mouth, and her legs sagged beneath her as he
took her breath away.

She clung to him obsessively, convinced now that her
destiny lay in his hands, and his mouth left hers to seek
her throat and the sensitive curve of her breast. He trailed
his tongue over her skin, leaving a dampness she hardly
noticed, and when he found her nipple he bit on it gently,
moistening the flimsy folds that were all that covered
her.

She was filled with an emotion she had never felt
before. Her limbs were weak, and yet every inch of her
was taut with longing for a fulfilment she sensed only
he could give her. Her thighs trembled; between her legs
the moist core of her femininity was proof—if any proof
were needed—that she wanted him just as much as he
wanted her. They were made for one another, and she
didn't care who knew it. If there were other dancers on
the terrace, let them look. She loved him, and she had
nothing to hide.

When he picked her up and laid her on a cushioned
swing, whose canopy gave only the scantest of protection, she knew he was going to make love to her. No:

not *to* her, *with* her, she thought sensuously. They would share the pleasure of their bodies. With a little cry of, '*Alex,*' she pulled him down on top of her, and wrapped her legs about him...

Camilla came awake with a start. She couldn't breathe, and she realised it was because she had wrapped herself around her pillow and her face was buried in its folds. She was hot, too; hot and sticky, her arms and legs slick with sweat.

But she knew it wasn't a fear of suffocation, or the fact that her nightgown was sticking to her, that had brought her awake. It was the dream she had been having, and the name she had called in those moments before her conscience had brought her back to reality, that had torn aside the veils of oblivion.

Trembling, she thrust the damp pillow aside, and, coming upright in the bed, she swept back her tumbled hair with an unsteady hand. Dear God, she thought sickly as the memory of the dream tumbled into her unwilling consciousness. She had been dreaming about Alex. And not just dreaming about him either, if the evidence of her shaking body was anything to go by. She had been *living* in her subconscious, and the waves of disappointment that were sweeping over her now were eloquent of her denial.

God! She thrust her legs over the side of the bed, and sat for several minutes with her head buried in her hands. This had never happened to her before, and all those stories she had heard and laughed about, of people actually being *aroused* by something they had dreamed, were no longer so funny. Her whole body was alive to the sexual fantasy she had conjured up, and the frustration she felt at its disintegration was just as real as the clammy texture of her skin.

Getting up from the bed, she crossed the carpet and went down the steps on to the cold wood floor. Her toes curled against its chilly surface, but the coolness that spread up her legs was welcome.

Drawing the curtain aside, she peeped outside and was rewarded by the faint glow on the horizon. She didn't know what time it was, but it was obvious it would soon be daylight, and she was relieved. She didn't think she could bear to get back into bed again and risk rekindling the emotions that had brought her awake. Apart from anything else, they were totally outrageous, not just because she hardly knew the man, but because he was Virginia's husband. And whatever kind of disaster his marriage had turned out to be she had no right to get involved. Besides, he hardly knew she was alive, she thought dully. She was just his link with Virginia, a particularly annoying thorn in his side who now and then aroused his frustration. But not his *sexual* frustration, she appended, feeling the first twinges of a headache assaulting her temples. Just an awareness of his delusion.

With a feeling of dejection, Camilla unlocked the sliding door and stepped out on to the balcony. The air was cool and refreshing, and she linked her fingers together and stretched her arms above her head. Her back muscles flexed obediently, and by the time she lowered her hands she was feeling minutely better. After all, it was only a dream, she told herself impatiently. All she had done was create an hallucination in which her subconscious had substituted some scene from the past. It wasn't as if she had never danced with a man before. She had done so, dozens of times. Granted, the kind of dancing she did most frequently did not resemble her dream, but recently one of the partners in the law firm for which she worked had taken her to a hunt ball in Gloucestershire. Of course, the dress she had worn then had been different, she remembered, recalling its sequined bodice with some pride. Though not as sexy, a small voice chided drily, and her spirits slumped again.

She couldn't help remembering how transparent the gown in her dream had been, and how she had been wearing nothing underneath it. Was that how she really wanted to appear to Alex Conti? she wondered unhappily. Was it only in her subconscious that she was completely honest with herself?

But he had thought she was beautiful, she reminded herself unwillingly. And she had never felt so sophisticated, or so desirable, before. No man had ever looked at her the way he had looked at her, even if it was only in her imagination. And no man had ever pressed himself against her so that the outline of his manhood felt as if it were still imprinted on her stomach.

Camilla's hand probed her flat stomach, quivering now, beneath the thin material of her nightgown. What would it feel like if Alex really held her like that? she pondered. If his hand explored her breasts and thighs, and his tongue explored her mouth...?

She brought herself up at that point. Standing on the balcony, swaying in the cool draught from the ocean, she was in danger of deluding herself that such a possibility might exist. It didn't. She was fooling herself if she believed that Alex would ever view her as anything more than a rather annoying intruder, whose connection to Virginia forced him to keep her here. She had had an example of how he felt about her the day before, when he had warned her not to leave the island, and, although he hadn't yet made good his threat to confiscate her passport, she had no doubt that he would, if necessary. As it was, there was a state of almost armed neutrality between them, and until Virginia made her next move there was nothing Camilla could do.

Virginia ...

Camilla stepped forward, her hands gripping the rail of the balcony as a sudden thought struck her. *Virginia had phoned her!* She had rung the house and asked to speak to her, when she had left home, not knowing if Camilla would come to the island. But she had rung the house, and stated that Camilla had been there for three days! How had she known? Who had told her?

Camilla blinked, the lingering lethargy of her dream dispersing as her brain came into action. Of course. She should have thought of that at once. It was only Alex's storming into the dining-room, disrupting her thought processes and scattering her wits, that had prevented her from seeing the obvious. Virginia had rung the house. It hadn't just been a lucky chance. She had actually had knowledge of Camilla's arrival.

Which meant only one thing: someone else knew where she was. Someone else, who knew Alex's movements, and her own, and who was reporting back to Virginia. But who?

Camilla tried to think. It couldn't be Mama Lu, or Wong Lee. She knew Alex could trust them with his life. So it was probably another of the servants. Or one of the security men.

She expelled her breath on a heavy sigh. If only she had thought of this before. It was something she could have told Alex without betraying her friend's confidence, and perhaps it would have persuaded him that she was not hiding anything. She had no more idea where Virginia was now than she had had before, and, if Alex had listened to the recording of their conversation, he must know that, too.

Thinking of the recording, Camilla shivered. She couldn't help remembering the callous way Virginia had spoken of her husband, and the shocking indifference she had shown towards his well-being. Not to mention the mocking aspersions she had made about his sexuality, she recalled guiltily. God, was that why she had had that dream about him? Because everything in her being cried out that Virginia was wrong?

Shaking her head, she turned back into her room and looked at the clock on the bedside table. It was after six, she saw with some relief, and if she wanted to catch Alex before he left for his office she might as well get ready. In spite of the fact that he had been so unpleasant yesterday, she was prepared to make amends, and as he had had supper at his parents' house the night before this would be her first opportunity to speak to him since that embarrassing débâcle.

She took more care with her appearance than usual, coiling her hair into a knot, instead of plaiting it as she had done before, and putting on a cotton dress instead of shorts. She told herself it was because she had more time than usual, and that it was just a way to fill in an hour or more until it was time for breakfast. But her conscience was less gullible than she had anticipated, and the annoying voice inside her insisted she was just riding for a fall.

However, when she emerged on to the terrace later, it was to find the breakfast table laid for one. Frowning, because it was only half-past seven and Mama Lu hadn't even brought her her morning tray of coffee yet, she

wondered if the setting was for her after all. Perhaps
Alex expected to get his breakfast and be gone before
she got up. That would explain the single glass and the
single cup and saucer.

Mama Lu's appearance disabused her of that thought.
When Camilla asked why the table had only been set for
one, the housekeeper explained that Mr Conti hadn't
come home the night before.

'Oh—not because he's had any more news of Mrs
Virginia,' she added when Camilla's eyes widened
anxiously. 'He just spent the night with his mom and
poppa. He said to tell you he'd be back later today.'

'Thanks.'

Camilla's response was unguardedly cynical, and
Mama Lu propped her hands on her ample hips and
regarded the younger woman consideringly. 'You got a
problem with that?'

'What? Oh, no.' Camilla was in no state to cross
swords with the housekeeper right now. 'Er—thank you
for telling me.'

'You're welcome.'

But Mama Lu didn't move away, and Camilla guessed
she had something more to say.

'You all right?' she asked after a moment, and Camilla
put up a hand to her throat, where the pale skin was so
revealing.

'I . . . yes. Yes, I'm fine.'

'You didn't eat much last night,' Mama Lu declared,
revealing that, although Wong Lee had served the meal,
she was still very much aware of what went on.

'No.' Camilla forced a polite smile now, and pointedly
took her seat at the table. 'Perhaps I'll do better this
morning.'

'You had a disagreement with Alex yesterday afternoon, didn't you?' the housekeeper persisted, clearly not
prepared to be intimidated by anyone. 'About the phone
call you took from Mrs Virginia. You should have told
him about it. Makes you look like a conspirator, if you
see what I mean.'

Camilla held up her head. 'Are you in the habit of
discussing your employer's affairs with his guests?' she

enquired in her most daunting tone, but Mama Lu merely shrugged.

'I just thought you ought to know that he took that real bad,' she replied carelessly. 'Seems like he trusted you to tell him if you had any word from Mrs Virginia, and you let him down.'

'Let him down?' Camilla snorted. 'I didn't let him down. How was I supposed to tell him anyway? He wasn't here.'

'You could have phoned his office.'

'Oh, yes? D'you think he would have wanted everyone there to know that his wife had phoned *me*?'

'When he came home, then?'

Camilla clenched her fists. 'I didn't get the chance.'

'Didn't you?'

'No.' Camilla refused to be intimidated in her turn. 'For heaven's sake, why does it matter anyway? He already knew all there was to know.'

'Mmm.' Mama Lu shrugged. 'So what did she say? It must have been something pretty bad to get him all riled up like that.'

Camilla caught her breath. 'If you think I'm going to discuss what——'

'She tell you why she ran away?'

'No.' Camilla refused to be drawn.

'How about their marriage, huh? Yeah, I guess that's what she'd tell you.' She paused, and then, apparently satisfied with what she could read from Camilla's expression, she went on, 'She tell you Alex doesn't care about her, yeah? That they have separate rooms? That he hasn't touched her in heaven knows how long?'

'Mama Lu, *please*!'

'OK, OK. You don't wanna talk about it. I can understand that. But, whatever she told you, you remember she married Alex 'cause she needed his money to subsidise that little habit of hers, *capisce*?'

Camilla swallowed. 'You don't know that for a fact.'

'Don't I?' Mama Lu's lips twisted. 'I've had to clear up after her plenty of times. I know, believe me. You ought to ask her about that mother of hers. Why she's locked up in that sanatorium in England. They say she's lucky to be alive, but, me, I'd rather be dead than living in some mental institution!'

'A mental institution!' Camilla was horrified, but Mama Lu only nodded.

'That's right. A mental institution. That's what it does to you, you know. If it doesn't destroy you physically it destroys your mind. And Alex has been paying to keep her in comparative luxury, since a couple of years after the wedding.'

Camilla couldn't believe it. 'But Virginia said——'

'Yes? What she say?'

'That...that her mother was ill.'

'She is.' The housekeeper grimaced. 'Like crazy as a loon, if you know what I mean.'

Camilla shook her head. 'I—I don't know what to say.'

'How about starting to believe Alex when he tells you he's going out of his mind with worry about Maria?'

Camilla lifted her shoulders. 'I do believe that.'

'And telling him anything you think might help him find her.'

'I have...that is...' Camilla moistened her lips '...I have thought of something. Will...will he be coming back here this morning?'

'I wouldn't think so.' Mama Lu frowned. 'You wanna tell me what it is?'

'I'd—rather tell him,' said Camilla, feeling the heat invade her cheeks at these words. 'Um—do you think he would mind if I went to his office?'

'To his office?' Mama Lu looked doubtful. 'He left instructions that you weren't to leave the estate——'

'What?'

Camilla gasped, and Mama Lu lifted her hands in a placating gesture. 'Now, don't you go getting all riled up about that. After what happened yesterday I guess he thought he had no alternative.'

'What do you mean?'

'Well—Mrs Virginia could call again, couldn't she?' said Mama Lu reasonably. 'And there's no saying what she'd ask you to do if he's not here.'

'Huh!' Camilla was unconvinced. She knew exactly why Alex had issued that instruction, and it had nothing to do with her well-being. He might not have taken her passport away from her, but he had done his best to ensure that she didn't leave the island until he said she could. Damn it! He couldn't do this to her.

'Anyway, you could call his office,' suggested the housekeeper after a moment. 'I'm sure if Alex thought you wanted to talk to him he'd come home——'

'No!'

'What do you mean?' Mama Lu spread her hands. 'If Alex doesn't want you to leave here there's no way——'

'Isn't there?' Camilla looked up at her, and now the light of determination was clearly visible in her eyes. 'I wonder what the local constabulary would have to say about confining a foreign national against her will?'

'The local constab…oh, you mean the cops?' Mama Lu shook her head. 'Now, you wouldn't do a thing like that, would you?'

'I might.' Camilla maintained her air of defiance, but she wondered if she would go that far. 'For God's sake,' she added, 'I'm not trying to run away! I just want to talk to…to Alex. One of the security men could drive me to his office, couldn't they? And wait to bring me back again, if you think that's necessary.'

'Well…' Mama Lu looked less sure of herself now. 'I guess that might be arranged.'

'Great!'

Camilla was relieved, but the housekeeper was still considering. 'I could ring Alex——'

'No.' Camilla sighed. 'Don't do that, please. I promise, you can trust me.'

'Can I?'

'You're going to have to,' said Camilla, with more assurance than she felt. 'And now, do you think I could have some French toast? And some coffee. I'm hungry. Really.'

CHAPTER NINE

WHETHER or not Mama Lu rang Alex to warn him, Camilla was determined to go into Honolulu, if only to prove to him that he couldn't dictate what she was to do and get away with it. Besides, she did want to talk to him without the constant spectre of distrust between them.

Although she had told Mama Lu she was hungry, it took a real effort to swallow the French toast the housekeeper brought for her. It entailed smothering it very thoroughly with maple syrup, and the thought of the number of calories she was eating was horrifying. But it was delicious, and it would have been a shame to disappoint the cook, whoever she was. In any case, she was probably going to burn off at least half the energy consumed in her coming confrontation with Alex. She was already in a state of nervous tension when Wong Lee came to tell her the car was waiting.

It was a black car, a stretch limousine, she supposed it was called, and resembled nothing so much as a hearse. The windows all appeared to be blacked out, too, but she discovered she could see out perfectly well from inside the vehicle. Very appropriate, Camilla thought ruefully, climbing into the back. At least the mood was appropriate anyway.

Her driver was one of the security guards—or she assumed he was. He was very smart, with closely cropped hair and a dark moustache. He was wearing an olive-green shirt with epaulettes, and there was a badge, with a number on it, pinned to his sleeve.

She caught him looking at her through the rear-view mirror as they drove towards the gates of the estate. She guessed he was wondering who she really was, and why he had been detailed to drive her to his employer's office. After all, she hadn't exactly been visible about the

112

grounds, and, although he probably knew her name, he was bound to be curious as to why she was still here.

Beyond the gates a noisy group of people jostled the car as it drove through, and Camilla was disturbed. It was only when she saw the expensive cameras slung about their necks that she realised who they were. It was obvious that Alex had not been successful in keeping Virginia's and Maria's disappearance from the Press, and Camilla's sympathies strengthened at this unwarranted intrusion. Alex had so much else to contend with, she thought. He could do without this invasion of his privacy.

She wondered who had told them, and then realised that, with so many employees, it would be virtually impossible to silence everyone. Besides, the Press paid well for that kind of information. Particularly about a man who didn't court a public image.

She had plenty of opportunity to admire the scenery as they drove into Honolulu, and this time she didn't miss the towering bulk of Diamond Head, or the twin towers of the Hyatt Regency Hotel that overlooked Waikiki Beach. Her driver took her right along Kalakaua Avenue, and it wasn't until they turned into the busy streets of the town that Camilla looked away from the ocean. There was so much to see: people swimming, and windsurfing; playing volley-ball on the beach; and of course the ubiquitous surfers, riding the foaming breakers right on to the sand. Holiday-makers, thought Camilla, half enviously, wishing she was one of them.

Tall buildings overshadowed the car as they drove into the business district of Honolulu. Jutting scaffolds indicated that more skyscrapers were being constructed, and the incongruity of seeing palm trees growing cheek-by-jowl with some concrete monstrosity struck Camilla as rather poignant. But there was an air of industry here, and the commercial section was buzzing with activity. Even so, many of the people she saw, men as well as women, going to and from their offices were dressed in the bright flamboyant colours for which Hawaii was famous, and she guessed they enjoyed brightening up their day.

The car eventually turned on to a coolly shadowed avenue with many official-looking buildings crowding the pavement. Camilla saw insurance companies, and stockbrokers, and several banks, before another cluster of reporters marked the entrance to the Conti building. Her heart sank. She had no wish to run the gamut of the Press, and she was much relieved when her driver turned into an underground garage, where another security barrier was raised to allow them in.

'You can take the elevator up to Mr Conti's office from here,' remarked the driver laconically, lowering the glass partition that had prevented her from speaking to him on their journey and turning to glance at her. 'Punch the button for the thirty-fifth floor. Mr Conti's staff will tell you if he can see you.'

'Oh—thank you.' Realising he was not about to open the door for her, Camilla pressed the handle herself and slid out. 'I—er—do I meet you here later?'

'Not me,' replied the driver, lowering his electrically controlled window when Camilla closed the car door. 'My orders are just to deliver you here. I guess Carlo will be detailed to bring you back.'

'Carlo?'

Camilla frowned, and the man explained. 'Carlo Ventura. Mr Conti's driver. Mama Lu said Mr Conti would deal with that. I got to get back to the estate.'

'I see.'

Camilla didn't really, but she had no wish to continue a conversation with someone who obviously regarded her as little better than the reporters at the gates. Who did Alex's staff think she was? she wondered. Apart from those who worked in the house, that was. She was pretty sure Mama Lu knew everything about her.

'OK. Be seeing you,' the man declared, raising his window again and successfully ending their exchange. Still, Camilla had been glad of the concealing blackness earlier, she conceded ruefully. She had no wish for her picture to appear in the tabloid Press.

The limousine glided away, and Camilla looked about her. She was surrounded by cars of all kinds, and she guessed this was where the staff who worked in the building left their vehicles. But she wasn't interested in car-spotting, even if one or two of the expensive-looking convertibles would have borne a second glance. Her task was to find the lift—no, elevator—to take her up to Alex's office. The thirty-fifth floor, she thought with a grimace. It promised to be quite a ride.

In the event, it only took a few seconds. The high-speed lift swept her up to the thirty-fifth floor in something less than a minute, and when she stepped out on to a carpeted landing she felt as if her stomach were still somewhere around the fourteenth.

Yet another security check awaited her. A black man this time, in a navy blue uniform and peaked cap that resembled the other uniform only in its uniformity. He occupied a desk in a plush reception area, and she was slightly disconcerted to see that he wore a revolver strapped to his hip.

However, she evidently offered no threat, and he was coolly polite when he enquired what her business was.

'Um—I'd like to see Mr Conti, please,' Camilla responded evenly, squeezing her clutch-bag between her fingers and holding it at the extent of her arms so that it successfully hid the few inches of pale thigh visible below the short hem of her skirt. 'My name's Camilla Richards, and he does know me.'

'You have an appointment, Miss Richards?'

He was about as giving as a concrete pillar, Camilla decided impatiently. But, 'No,' she conceded, losing patience with her own diffidence, and tucking her bag beneath her arm. 'However, if you tell him I'm here, I'm sure you'll find he'll see me. I'm—I'm his house guest. I'm staying out at Kumaru.'

'Yes, Miss Richards.' Whether he believed her or not, she couldn't be sure, but what she was not prepared for was for him to hold out his hand and gesture at her clutch-bag. 'Then you won't mind if I check you don't have a recorder in there, will you?' he added. 'If you don't mind. I have my orders.'

'Haven't we all?' muttered Camilla irritably, but, after the gaggle of reporters she had seen downstairs, she supposed she could understand his caution. But for heaven's sake, did she look like a reporter? Where was her notebook and camera?

Her bag successfully checked for bugs, the man picked up a telephone and apparently dialled Alex's office. Camilla tried not to listen to his conversation, sure that if she did she would feel even more frustrated than she already did. However, she couldn't avoid hearing the word 'allegedly', and it didn't take much imagination to guess what he was saying.

Still, contrary to her growing expectations, she wasn't asked to leave. Instead, after finishing his phone call, the man invited her to sit on one of the velvet couches that lined the silk-hung walls of the reception area, and her unwilling guardian resumed his seat at his desk.

A few moments later a pretty Chinese girl came through a door at the end of the corridor that stretched away from the reception area, and walked towards them. She was small and slim and exotic-looking, with chin-length hair that tipped under her jawline, and small oriental features.

'Miss Richards,' she said, and, although her appearance was foreign, her accent was not. She had obviously been born and bred in the United States, and it showed both in her manner and her style of dress. 'I'm Sophy Ling. Will you come with me, please?'

Camilla got to her feet gratefully, feeling none the less something of a giant as she accompanied the diminutive Miss Ling back along the corridor. Still, she was glad the pale green shift she was wearing was reasonably elegant. Like many of her countrywomen, Sophy was immaculately turned out.

'You are on holiday, Miss Richards?' she asked, as they trod the pale grey broadloom, and, although Camilla guessed she was just being polite, she was wary of saying anything that might incriminate her.

'Um . . . sort of,' she said, letting it be known that she was not eager to explain her reasons for being there, and Sophy looked at her appraisingly as she reached the inner door.

Beyond the door another office awaited her. This was much bigger than the reception area, however, and there were long windows with vertical blinds to filter the intrusive rays of the sun. A quartet of desks, two equipped with computers and two with electronic typewriters, were

set at right angles to each other, apparently providing a
working base for Sophy and another girl, who was presently engaged in earnest conversation with the man
leaning over her desk. It wasn't until he straightened that
Camilla realised it was Grant Blaisdell, and it took an
enormous effort not to let her disappointment show.

'Well, well, well, what have we here?' he exclaimed,
coming round the desk and looking her over very
thoroughly. 'If it isn't the fair Camilla, come to beard
the lion in his den. You didn't say we were expecting a
visitor, Sophy. I wondered why you went dashing off
like that.'

The expression Sophy cast in Grant's direction mirrored her own, and Camilla felt a corresponding warming
in her attitude towards the Chinese girl. The second girl,
who was fairly plump with straight silky-blonde hair that
fell to her shoulders, was watching the exchange with
interest, and it was obvious from her expression that she
regarded Grant with far more enthusiasm.

'We weren't, Mr Blaisdell,' Sophy responded now,
waiting until Grant had released Camilla's unwilling hand
before continuing, 'but, as you evidently know Miss
Richards, I think I ought to let Mr Conti know she's
here. He's in conference with Mr Cassells, but I'm sure
he won't mind being interrupted.'

'That won't be necessary,' declared Grant, putting his
hand over Sophy's as it reached for the phone on her
desk. That she extracted her fingers immediately didn't
seem to faze him. He had achieved his objective, and
that was all that mattered. 'I'll tell Alex Camilla's here.
But first, I'm sure she wouldn't say no to some coffee.
We'll have it in my office, Sophy. Oh, and send one of
the girls out for a Danish, hmm? Cream cheese for me.
How about you, Camilla?'

Camilla ignored Grant and looked at Sophy. 'If you
don't mind I'll wait until Mr Conti is free,' she said
evenly. 'Is it all right if I go back to Reception?'

There was a moment's silence while Sophy absorbed
what she had said and Grant and the other girl ex-
changed glances. And then, as if on cue, the double doors
at the far side of the office opened, and two men came
into the room. One of them was in his sixties, Camilla

surmised, a rather fatherly looking figure with a shock
of grey hair and horn-rimmed spectacles; the other was
Alex.

The two men had been talking as they came through
the doors, but the lack of activity in the outer office
caused both of them to look up in surprise. They saw
the four figures standing like statues, and Alex's eyes
went straight to Camilla.

But, predictably, it was Grant who was first to recover.
'Hey, you've got a visitor, Alex!' he exclaimed,
glancing at Camilla as if she hadn't just turned down
his offer of hospitality. 'Is there anything I can do?'

Alex's expression was unreadable. Oh, he offered
Grant a casual smile, and appeared to be considering the
merits of what the other man had said, but Camilla
sensed that they were not penetrating the mask of neutrality he was presently maintaining. None of them knew
what he was really thinking, she thought uneasily, not
really understanding how she should know that. But the
fact was, she did, and she waited expectantly for him to
speak.

'I'll get to you later, Jim,' he said in an aside to his
companion, and then came across the room to where
Camilla was standing. 'Hi. This is an . . . unexpected . . .
pleasure.'

Camilla managed a smile, but she didn't know how
she did it. And it wasn't just because Grant, the other
man and the two secretaries were watching them, she
acknowledged tensely. In spite of her efforts to push all
thought of the night before to the back of her mind,
seeing Alex in the flesh again tore down all the barriers
she had erected. It was impossible to look at him without
remembering what she had dreamed he had done to her—
and her response. It was all still too vivid in her mind,
and it took an actual physical effort to separate the substance from the fantasy.

'I suggest we go into my office,' Alex said after a moment's consideration, and Camilla was grateful. At least
she wouldn't be in any danger of making a fool of herself
in front of anyone else, she thought wryly. She would
just have to hope she didn't do the same with Alex. She

was half afraid to look at him in case he guessed what she was thinking.

She gave Sophy a faintly rueful look before accompanying him out of the room, and was rewarded by a matching grin. At least she had one ally, she thought as she followed Alex through the panelled doors, which she now saw led into his office. And she obviously wasn't the only female who found Grant Blaisdell's attentions repulsive.

Alex waited by the doors until she had passed through them, then closed them behind him and leaned back against the wood. 'Well?' he said, and for a moment she thought he was challenging her. 'I gather you've got some news.'

Camilla swallowed. He wasn't. But it was obvious her appearance here hadn't been as much a surprise to him as she had anticipated. 'Er—how do you know that?' she asked evasively, playing for time. This was Virginia's husband, remember? she told herself furiously. Sexually, he doesn't even know you exist!

'Call it intuition,' Alex responded now, and Camilla drew a steadying breath.

'Aided and abetted by Mama Lu, no doubt,' she countered, and Alex shrugged.

'You didn't really expect her to sanction your leaving the house without consulting me, did you?'

Camilla sighed. 'I suppose not.'

'There you are, then.' Alex straightened away from the door, and walked across to his desk. In shirt-sleeves and dark tan trousers, he passed quite close to where she was standing, and involuntarily she drew back. 'So... why all the cloak and dagger? Couldn't you have told Mama Lu?'

That hurt. But it also had the effect of bringing her to her senses. 'I could have, yes,' she agreed shortly. 'But I thought—foolishly, as it turns out—that you'd prefer me not to discuss your affairs with an employee!'

'Mama Lu's hardly an employee,' retorted Alex, equally as brusquely. 'She's lived at the estate since before I was born, and she's practically *family*!'

'Which I'm not,' Camilla remarked tersely, only wanting to get out before she said or did something she would regret. 'All right. I'll discuss my ideas with Mama Lu.' She turned to walk away. 'I'm sorry I intruded——'

'Oh, for God's sake!' Although her legs were long, his were longer, and he overtook her easily, before she reached the doors. His fingers closed about her upper arm. 'Where d'you think you're going?' he exclaimed impatiently, swinging her round to face him. 'You're here now, so you might as well spit it out!'

Camilla steeled herself to look up at him, and when she did her eyes were as green as glass, and just as giving. 'The only spitting I'm likely to do is at you, Mr Conti,' she told him angrily. 'Now, let go of my arm, before I really show my claws!'

'Camilla . . .'

Alex was frustrated, but he wasn't letting her go, and Camilla wanted to scream. Perhaps she should, she thought consideringly. She was sure that would get his attention. But she wasn't an hysterical person in the usual way, and she was already fighting to remember who she really was.

'Are you going to let go of me?' she demanded, looking up at him now with eyes that glistened with the threat of tears, and her heart constricted. Dear God, she thought despairingly, this couldn't be happening to her; it really couldn't. She didn't get herself into this sort of situation. She simply wasn't the type to be governed by her emotions.

'All right, all right.' Alex released her arm abruptly and thrust his hands into his trousers pockets. But his expression was by no means impassive, and a pulse was jumping at his jawline as he endeavoured to control his own feelings. 'However, I don't think there's any need for us to maintain this aggression, do you? You'll have to forgive me if I'm on edge. I do have a lot on my plate at the moment.'

Camilla swallowed. 'If you say so,' she responded rather ungraciously, but she couldn't help it. Her own nerves were tearing her to ribbons, and she found his politeness almost more than she could bear.

'Good.' He was making an obvious effort to pace himself. 'So—what did you come to tell me?'

Camilla shrugged. Her reasons for being here had lost all importance, and she wished he would move away from her. He was too damned close for comfort, and her pulse was already behaving erratically, causing all sorts of problems with her breathing. Why didn't he go back to his desk and allow them both to get their breaths back— metaphorically and physically? Why did he persist in standing over her, disrupting not only her metabolism, but her ability to think rationally?

'Camilla?'

His repeated use of her name was hoarse, and her head came up with a start. There had been an almost desperate note in his voice as he'd spoken, and, when her eyes encountered his, her mouth dried. He wasn't looking at her as if he resented her invasion of his office. He wasn't even looking at her as if he was impatient for her to answer him. Instead, his face was taut with emotion, and her knees shook as she struggled to keep her head.

Her lips parted, but the words that might have issued from them were never spoken. As if the sight of that tremulous separation and the tender pink tip of tongue that appeared to moisten them was the final straw, Alex dragged his hands out of his pockets and grasped her shoulders. The sure touch of his hands sent her senses reeling, and when he jerked her towards him she had no will to resist him. His mouth fastened on hers, and substance and fantasy blended into one all-consuming assault on her emotions.

His kiss was hard at first, rough and aggressive, as if he was demonstrating his own reluctance to give in to what was, of course, only a fleeting aberration. He hadn't intended to touch her, Camilla realised dizzily. He had believed he could control his feelings, and even when he took hold of her he had intended it to be a kind of punishment—as well as proving to himself that the situation was not getting out of hand.

But it didn't work that way. As soon as his lips touched hers, Camilla's mouth opened, and his tongue slid almost involuntarily between her teeth. And at once the kiss softened and deepened, so that Camilla emitted a helpless little moan before responding completely.

Her hands, which had been trapped between their bodies, spread over the warm flesh, palpable beneath the thin material of his shirt, and then moved up to clutch the sides of his neck. Her body arched towards him, and his hands slid up her arms to her wrists, before taking them behind her back and using them to urge her hips against his. His thumbs caressed her palms as he compelled her closer, and she felt the heat of her lower spine against her knuckles as he increased the pressure.

But it was the heat of his body that caused the blood to rise to the surface of her skin; the rampant sexuality of his kiss that blotted out all but the urgent need to press herself even closer. Their clothes were a tormenting barrier to the freedom she desired, and moisture pooled between her breasts and trickled down her back. He released her hands to slide his fingers over her hips to her waist, and from there across the curve of her ribcage. His hands clung to the damp cotton of her dress, and she felt the hemline lifting as his exploration reached her breasts. His mouth left hers then, to trail a moist path to her shoulder, and his thumbs brushed her swollen nipples, where they thrust shamelessly against the cloth.

He was going to make love to her: she knew it. His leg was between hers, the bones of his pelvis taut and unyielding. But it was the heaviness that was becoming tangible between his legs that convinced her, the pulsating tumescence that strained the zip of his trousers and throbbed against her stomach. And this was no dream, she reminded herself harshly, striving for sanity: this was real; this was Alex; and he was still Virginia's husband.

CHAPTER TEN

'No,' CAMILLA got out unsteadily, when Alex's fingers went to the buttons of her bodice, and, although he opened the first two of them, it was a purely reflex action. Already her trembling denial had brought him at least partly to his senses, and, although he didn't step away from her, his hands fell automatically to his sides. It enabled Camilla to put some space between them, and she dried her damp palms by smoothing them down over her hips. The action also restored her hemline to some-where near its proper position, and she kept her eyes averted the whole time.

The silence in the room was crippling, and as Camilla secured her buttons again she strove desperately for some lightweight comment. She ought to be able to think of something, she chafed, wetting her lips and then with-drawing her tongue again as she remembered what had happened the last time she had made such a provocative gesture. Only it hadn't been intended to be provocation, she defended herself unhappily. The trouble was, such experience as she had had with men had not prepared her for the kind of violent reaction she had to Alex. Although she had been kissed before—and more, she acknowledged ruefully—she had never experienced any-thing like the frenzy of feeling Alex had aroused.

She felt like a virgin, she thought fretfully, and he probably thought she was one, too. After all, she was almost thirty, and unmarried, with no visible man on her horizon. It would be quite natural for him to think she had never slept with a man, and her quivering re-fusal had had all the prudery of a maiden aunt. He couldn't know that in her second year at college—and egged on by the fear of being thought prudish by her peers—she had lost her virginity to a young man who was reputed to be quite a stud. That the young man in

123

question had only gained his reputation by sleeping with
most of the female population of the university had soon
become apparent. His careless invasion of her body had
left Camilla cold, and thereafter she had kept her relationships with other students on a casual basis only.

Of course, since starting work there had been other
friendships, some of them more serious than others, but
sex had never figured very highly in her relationships.
She knew that some of the men she had gone out with—
and who she had refused to go to bed with—thought
her cold, but it wasn't that. Her experience, and it was
of necessity small, had not led her to believe she was
destined for some earth-shattering love-affair. She had
expected to get married some day, but more for com-
panionship and children than for any other reason. Now
she realised how wrong she had been. When Alex kissed
her she turned to fire, and the thought of making love
with him melted every bone in her body.

But he was Virginia's husband, she chided herself
again. Dear God, the man was desperate! Otherwise, he
never would have touched her.

When the phone rang she started violently. She had
been so wrapped up with her thoughts, and the self-
denigrating memory of her own complicity in what had
obviously been an embarrassing mistake, that she had
almost forgotten where she was. Alex's move to answer
it was a daunting reminder, and she would have let herself
out of the room as he did so if he hadn't pressed a button
on the console and said roughly, 'Wait!'

Then, releasing the button, he spoke to whomever it
was on the other end of the line. Propped on a corner
of his desk, one foot raised off the floor, the other supporting his weight, he seemed in complete control of
himself again, and Camilla realised she had the time it
took for him to finish his call for her to gather her own
scattered wits. If she could meet his gaze without her
conscience getting in the way she might do it, too, she
thought manfully. The trouble was, her conscience wasn't
as easy to manipulate as his evidently was.

'No,' Alex was saying now, and, as the awareness of
where she was and what she was doing here took pre-
cedence, Camilla couldn't help listening to what he was

saying. 'Yes. Here in Honolulu,' he conceded flatly. 'No, I don't think there's any point in your staying out there. Yes. As soon as you get back.'

He replaced the receiver then, and his eyes, which had flickered in her direction from time to time during his call, turned on her. At some point during the call he had unbuttoned the collar of his shirt and loosened his tie, and she guessed that, in spite of his apparent control now, his temperature had coincided with hers. She hadn't imagined the heavy heat of his arousal, and her eyes skipped nervously over the tan cloth that covered his thighs. But, although his position on the desk necessarily tautened the fine material across his hips, there was no evidence now of his bulging sex. Like his ardour, it had subsided, and Camilla quivered with something approaching disappointment.

'Don't,' he said abruptly, and, although she was now staring somewhat zealously through the windows of the office, she knew exactly what he meant.

But she couldn't tell him that. 'I beg your——?' she was beginning, when he interrupted her.

'You came to tell me something,' he said flatly. 'If you can forget what just happened, and tell me what that was, I'd be grateful.'

I'd bet you would, thought Camilla indignantly, but she knew it was an uncalled-for emotion. Of course he wanted her to forget what had happened. He wanted to forget it himself, and he couldn't do that if she turned out to be one of those women who laboured a situation to death. And it would have been so easy to be one of those women, she acknowledged unhappily. What had happened had affected her more than she cared to examine, and it would have been so satisfying to throw it up at him and demand that he at least show some responsibility for what he had done.

Still, her legal training stood her in good stead at that moment, and, like the cool, unemotional advocate she had believed herself to be until a few moments ago, she schooled her features and allowed her gaze to come to rest slightly below his jaw. 'It . . . it was something I realised this morning,' she replied, endeavouring to keep the tremor out of her voice. 'When . . . when Virginia phoned she said I'd been at the house for . . . for three days.'

'Yes?'

'Well . . .' Camilla's voice cracked, and she had to clear her throat before continuing. 'How . . . how did she know? I mean—she said she ran away because . . . because she wasn't sure I would come. And yet . . . and yet . . .'

'She was fairly confident that you'd be there to answer her call,' finished Alex drily, and Camilla nodded.

'Yes.' Her shoulders sagged at his expression. 'I suppose you'd already noticed that.'

Alex hesitated. 'I'm—grateful to you for pointing it out.'

'But you knew, didn't you?' Camilla sighed. 'And I thought I'd made some exciting progress!' She shook her head. 'I should have known.'

'Why . . . progress?' Alex asked now, and, aware that he was watching her rather intently, Camilla shifted her weight from one foot to the other.

'Well . . .' She lifted her shoulders expressively. 'It's obvious, isn't it?'

'Is it?'

'Of course.' Camilla frowned, and darted a quick glance up at his dark face. 'Someone must have told her I was there, mustn't they?' She blinked. 'You surely don't think that it was me?'

'Don't be ridiculous!'

His response was dismissive, and Camilla's resentment stirred anew. Did he have to treat her as if she were a retarded child? How the hell was she supposed to know what he was thinking? She didn't even know what she was thinking herself.

As if realising he had been unnecessarily rude, Alex sighed, and, bending forward, he raked both hands through his hair. 'I just wanted to be sure that you'd come to the same conclusion as me,' he said wearily. 'I'm sorry if I offended you. It's just another item to add to the score.'

Camilla's resentment dissipated. She couldn't blame him really. Not when she had been as guilty as he had. She had wanted him to kiss her. She had been wanting him to kiss her ever since she'd come into the office.

And if she was painfully honest she had been aware of him ever since her arrival on the island.

'So...so has it helped in any way?' she ventured, wanting to get their relationship back on a normal footing, and, although Alex looked at her through narrowed eyes, his reply was as impassive as her question.

'The call helped a lot,' he said, straightening his spine with an obvious effort. 'Hell—you might as well know; Virginia phoned you from here, in Honolulu. It seems our discovery that a woman and child answering their descriptions had left the island was a deliberate attempt to mislead us. That's why we haven't been able to find them in San Diego. Virginia and Maria were never there.'

Camilla caught her breath. 'You mean—it was all planned?'

'It looks that way.'

'But...' Camilla shook her head bewilderedly. 'Why did she write to me, then?'

Alex's mouth compressed. 'That seems to be the only confusing factor. Why would she write to you if she was planning on abducting Maria?'

Camilla swallowed. 'I hope you're not thinking I made it up.'

'No.' Alex was impatient. 'For God's sake, Camilla, have I implied I think you might be involved?'

'Perhaps not——'

'Look, Virginia wrote to you. I accept that.' Alex breathed heavily. 'But it was out of character; surely you can see that? And phoning you yesterday—that was odd, too. Why would she deliberately blow her cover, just to hear your voice?'

'Blow her cover?' Camilla was surprised. 'But I thought you said you didn't have a trace on the call.'

'I didn't.' Alex paused. 'There were other giveaways. Not least the fact that there was no time-lag between her speaking and your answering.'

'And should there have been?'

'If she were on the mainland, yes. Not a lot, maybe, but enough to be noticeable. And, because this is an island, there's no way she could have faked it.'

'And that's it?'

'No.' Alex sighed. 'All phone time is registered. If you've ever made an international call you'll have heard it ticking away, every ten seconds or so. Virginia's call was clear.'

'I see.' Camilla was impressed. 'So, in other words, you believe she never left the island.'

'I'm sure of it.'

'Then, why——?'

'To give them time; to mislead us.'

'Them?'

'Well, as you pointed out, she must have had an ac-complice, mustn't she?' Alex countered grimly. 'I wonder if he approved of her calling you?'

'*He?*' Camilla hesitated. 'You're sure it's a man?'

'Aren't you? Can you see Virginia doing all this for a woman?' His mouth twisted. 'No. Don't answer that. It's not fair to expect you to make a judgement. You don't know her as I do.'

Camilla caught her lower lip between her teeth. He was right, of course. And the bitter woman she had spoken to on the phone bore little resemblance to the girl she had first got to know. Nevertheless, Virginia had written to her; she had phoned. She still expected some loyalty from their friendship; and Camilla had her own guilt to contend with now.

Looking about her, she saw her clutch-bag lying on the floor where it had fallen when Alex had taken her in his arms. Bending to pick it up, she determinedly tried to put all thoughts of that episode out of her mind, but it wasn't easy. All the time they had been talking, it had been there between them, like some unacknowledged crime they had committed. She didn't know what he was feeling. How could she? He was far better than she was at hiding his feelings. But she couldn't forget it, and she doubted she ever would. Which was why she had to get out of here—not just out of Alex's office, but off the island. Away from temptation, she admitted honestly, which Virginia's continued absence could only aggravate.

'I'd better go,' she said, tucking her bag under her arm and striving for a casual departure. 'It's almost lunchtime.'

Alex looked at her. 'Are you hungry?'

'No.' Camilla was honest. 'No, not especially.' She managed a strained smile. 'But I'm sure you have work to do, and ... and ...'

Alex got up from the desk. 'I'll arrange for a car——'

'No. No, don't do that.' Camilla's palms were moist again, and she surreptitiously dried them on her dress. 'I—er—as I'm in Honolulu I'd like to visit the airline office and find out if they've had any luck with my booking. I—well, I forgot to tell you, I phoned them yesterday morning. Before ... before Virginia rang. They've—er—they've put my name on stand-by.'

'Have they?' Alex regarded her without expression. 'Is that wise?'

'Wise?' Camilla was taken aback. 'Why not?'

Alex took a deep breath. 'I thought we'd discussed this, Camilla. I thought we'd agreed that you'd stay on until we found out exactly what it is Virginia does want.'

No.' Camilla shook her head. 'I mean—that wasn't agreed at all. I ... I know what you said, but ... well ... circumstances——'

'Haven't changed,' said Alex flatly. 'I thought you understood that, too. What ... happened ... was a mistake. I mean, we're all pretty uptight right now and, God knows, it shouldn't have happened. But it did.' He paused to take a breath, and then went on, 'Nevertheless, that doesn't alter the basic situation. Until I get some definite news of Virginia's whereabouts, I want you to stay here.'

'That's impossible.' Camilla was flabbergasted. 'I ... I have ... commitments——'

'Where? In England?' Patently, Alex didn't believe her. 'As I understand it, you came out here at Virginia's invitation for a holiday. *A holiday*, Camilla! In my book, that constitutes more than a couple of days.'

'Maybe so.' Camilla could feel a sense of panic rising inside her. 'But—oh, for goodness' sake, surely you can see that I can't stay here now?'

'Why not?'

'Why not?' She stared at him incredulously. 'You know why not!'

'Because of just now.' It wasn't a question. 'Don't be silly, Camilla.' Alex was infuriatingly calm. 'You're not a schoolgirl. It's not as if I violated some sacred trust.' His lips twisted. 'Or an innocent, for that matter. As I recall it, you didn't exactly fight me off.'

Camilla choked. 'You're still Virginia's husband,' she declared doggedly, unable to deny what was so obviously the truth. 'And...and I'm supposed to be her friend!'

'And that's what all this outraged indignation is about? Because I'm her husband, and you feel some latent sense of loyalty towards her?'

'Is that so unusual?' Camilla held up her head. 'I...I'm not in the habit of betraying my friends!'

'Oh, come on.' He shifted restlessly. 'Have you forgotten that call she made, because, if you have, I haven't. How was it she put it? Something about not objecting if you and I got it together. Or words to that effect, anyway.'

'I don't care what Virginia said.' Camilla squeezed her bag between her hands. 'And...and if you insist on bringing up that call perhaps I should remind you of my answer.'

'There's no need.' Alex seemed weary of the whole discussion. 'All right, give me a few minutes and I'll take you for some lunch. Maybe we can make some sense of this situation when we've both had a chance to cool off——'

'No, thanks.' Camilla walked towards the door, and although her confidence was not as sure as it appeared he made no move to follow her. 'I don't think there's any point in continuing this. I...I'll let you know if I have any luck with the airline.'

'But you will go back to the house?'

Alex's voice was low and controlled, and Camilla paused, with her fingers on the handle, to look back over her shoulder. 'I'll have to, won't I?' she retorted, and then let herself out of the room before he could say anything else.

An hour later she was sitting in a fast-food restaurant on Kalakaua Avenue which overlooked the crowded

sands of Waikiki. The burger she had ordered sat con-
gealing in its cardboard carton, and only the rather bitter
coffee they had provided had held any appeal. In consequence, the beaker was empty, and she was wishing she
had had the foresight to order herself a second cup. As
it was, there was a long queue at the counter, and the
distinct possibility that she would lose the seat she was
presently occupying if she left it. The restaurant was
buzzing with activity, and she had been lucky to find
somewhere to sit in the first place. That was why she
was loath to abandon it.

Still, she couldn't face looking at the burger for much
longer. Already its smell was curdling her stomach, and
it wasn't fair to deny someone else the chance to sit at
the table. She had no intention of eating it, but if she
left the restaurant she would have to face the prospect
of returning to Kumaru, and right now that was equally
uninviting.

If only she had had the sense to take the cancellation
when it was offered to her, she reflected bitterly. That
was really why she was sitting here, brooding over her
burger, and putting off the moment when she would have
to accept what she had done. Because when the girl in
the airline office had told her she could get her on
tomorrow morning's flight she had turned it down. No
matter how ridiculous it might sound to her now, when
the uniformed representative of the airline had told her
she had a cancellation booking to offer, Camilla had
panicked. Instead of jumping at the chance to leave the
island, she had made some puerile excuse about coming
into the office to take her name *off* the stand-by list.
She'd said she'd changed her mind about leaving, and
at this moment the seat she might have occupied was
probably being offered to someone else. *Crazy!*

'Do you mind if I join you?'

Camilla's head jerked up. A young man was standing
by her table, a tray containing a burger, fries, and a Coke
in his hands.

'Oh, I—no.'

Camilla got automatically to her feet, but the man's
bulk blocked her exit. 'Don't leave on my account,' he

said, his eyes warm and admiring. 'Can't we just share the table?'

Camilla's expression froze. 'I was just leaving,' she said, and something in her gaze must have warned him not to argue. 'Excuse me.' She brushed past him. 'Enjoy your meal.'

Outside again, the heat assaulted her lungs, and she expelled air in an upward stream over her face. It was hot; very hot; and, although she had thought of going sightseeing, what she really fancied was a nice cold shower. Or a dip in the ocean, she conceded ruefully, remembering how delightful that had been the day before. If she went back to the house she could change into her swim-suit and take a dip before Alex came home.

But the idea of going back to the house, of giving in to his demands, was not appealing. What was she going to say when he asked her whether she had managed to get a seat on the plane? Was she going to tell him she had turned down a chance to leave the island? Or pretend there had been no cancellation, and run the risk of his finding out that there had been later?

Either one was anathema to her. After her bravado of a couple of hours ago, he was bound to think either that he had intimidated her, or that she had changed her mind about their relationship. He might even think she was hoping to extend what had happened that morning. After all, he had implied that he believed Virginia's evaluation of her lifestyle. He might even believe she had some personal motive for seeking to prolong her visit.

'God!' Camilla shook her head despairingly, and turned right towards the towering hotels that faced the ocean. What was she going to do? She was in an impossible position.

The cooling shadows of the Hemmeter Centre beckoned, and, abandoning any decisions for the time being, Camilla turned into the exclusive shopping arcade. She had noticed it when she had passed the Hyatt Regency Hotel earlier, and now she rode the escalator to the first floor, where a gallery of fashionable boutiques overlooked a tumbling waterfall.

It was very peaceful, walking along the colonnade, looking in the windows of the different stores. For a few moments she could fool herself that she was just another tourist enjoying the anticipation of having money to spend and so many exciting things to spend it on. She even found herself admiring a navy blue dress, whose strappy bodice merged into a soft swinging skirt, appliquéd with elegant white flowers. It was exactly the kind of dress that, in other circumstances, she would have liked to buy. But right now she didn't even have the heart to ask how much it was. Besides, if she had to ask the price, she probably couldn't afford it, she reflected wryly. And expensive evening dresses were not very high on her shopping-list at the moment.

Walking on, she glanced over the balcony rail, and saw that several tables were set around the base of the waterfall on the ground floor. It was a rather attractive coffee-shop cum bar, with many of the customers enjoying the tall fruit-laden cocktails that were so much a part of the Hawaiian experience. It reminded Camilla that she had had no lunch, and, although she still wasn't particularly hungry, she was thirsty.

Taking the escalator down again, she walked between the palm-filled planters and found herself a table set against the basin of the waterfall. A long-haired Polynesian girl, dressed in an exotically coloured garment that resembled nothing so much as a short sari, came to take her order, and after consulting the menu Camilla chose a locally mixed cocktail. It was a Chi-chi, and when it came she found it tasted a little like a Pina Colada. Only the spirit used was vodka, and not rum, and in consequence the flavour of the pineapple juice was sweeter and more pungent.

It was delicious and, sipping it through the straw that was provided, Camilla allowed the holiday atmosphere of the sunlit courtyard to envelop her. She didn't even feel any resentment when someone else came to share her table. Live and let live, she thought inconsequently. At least it was another woman, she saw, her averted gaze taking in the slim legs and tight-fitting skirt of the newcomer. She wouldn't have to give her the brush-off, she conceded, and then was momentarily stunned when the woman nudged Camilla's knee with her own.

Oh, no! She groaned disgustedly. Not that! Why had she attracted that kind of attention? Couldn't a woman enjoy a drink, on her own, without some pervert thinking she was desperate for some company?

She looked up, her hand going automatically to the stem of her glass. She was quite prepared to use the glass as a weapon, if necessary, but when she focused on the intruder her whole body went limp.

'Virginia?' she said unbelievingly. 'My God, Virginia, is that you?'

CHAPTER ELEVEN

'Ssh, keep your voice down, for goodness' sake!'

The woman sitting opposite Camilla glanced half fearfully about her, and raised one hand in a warning gesture. As she did so, the black veil that completely shrouded her head and shoulders floated ethereally about her, giving Camilla the momentary illusion that none of this was quite real.

'Virginia——'

'Please don't use my name,' the woman implored warningly, leaning towards her across the table. 'Someone might hear you. Someone might recognise me. I'm not supposed to be here. He would kill me if he knew.'

'Alex?' Camilla frowned. 'I'm sure you're wrong.'

'Alex?' For a moment Virginia seemed puzzled, and then she shook her head. 'Oh, well, never mind that now. I needed to speak to you, Camilla. That's why I'm here.'

'But how did you find me?'

For the moment Camilla could only think of inconsequential details, and Virginia sighed. 'I knew you were at the office. Don't ask me how, I just did. I ... was waiting when you came out of the Conti building. I've been following you ever since.'

Camilla was stunned. It was difficult to assimilate the fact that Virginia was actually sitting here, talking to her. After the past few days, when her and the child's possible whereabouts had been paramount in everyone's mind, it was hard to believe she was not just a figment of her imagination. But it was Virginia, albeit much thinner than Camilla remembered, her thin claw-like hands opening and closing against the edge of the table, her features practically obscured by the funereal veil. She might not have wanted to be recognised, but her appearance had certainly attracted attention. Camilla could only assume she was more desperate than any of them had realised.

'Don't you think you should let Alex know where you are?' she ventured now, and Virginia sighed.

'Doesn't he know?' She sounded bitter, her nails beating a rapid tattoo against the surface of the table. 'I should have guessed he'd have the phone bugged when I rang you. But—it was a risk I had to take.'

Camilla put out her hand. 'Virginia—you need help——'

'Oh, yes, I need help all right!' exclaimed the other woman, flinching away from Camilla's touch. 'That's why I need you. You're the only person I can trust.'

Camilla caught her lower lip between her teeth. She was no expert, but she could see that Virginia wasn't well. Her hands, when they were not engaged in the agitated tapping, shook, her skin was unnaturally pale, even allowing for the veil, and she was ultra-sensitive to being touched. The classic symptoms of someone who was badly in need of a fix, she thought anxiously. Oh, God, if only Alex were here! But then, if he were, Virginia wouldn't be.

'Don't...don't try psychoanalysing me, Cam,' Virginia said now, her voice low but with an underlying note of hysteria. 'I don't have much time, and there's so much you must know.'

'Vir——' Camilla bit off the name. 'Please, you must let Alex help you.'

'Alex?' Virginia snorted. 'You really think Alex would help me now?'

'He has before,' said Camilla quietly, and Virginia's eyes flashed with a momentary trace of anger.

'So—he has been talking about me, has he?' she declared, twisting her hands together until the knuckles were white and tortured. 'Did he tell you he hates me? Was that how the story began?'

'No.' Camilla sighed. 'Vir...he doesn't hate you. He just—wants you to come back.'

'You mean, he wants Maria back,' contradicted Virginia cynically, and for a moment she was perfectly calm. 'Well, you can tell him he can have her. But only on my terms.'

Camilla stared at her. 'Oh, Virginia!'

'Don't look at me like that. As if you pity me. I don't need your pity, Camilla. Pity's impractical. I need your help.'

'Why?'

'Why?' Virginia tipped her head back against her shoulders for a second, and drew several gulping breaths. 'That's a good question, Cam. But I don't know if I can answer it.'

'Try.'

Virginia's chin dropped to her chest. 'Oh—it's a long story. You don't really want to hear it.'

'Look, I *am* interested; try me.'

'OK, I'll explain, but I know you won't approve.' Virginia took a deep breath. 'I married Alex for his money. And we didn't live happily ever after.'

Camilla frowned. 'But you had Maria.'

'Yes, we had Maria.' Virginia's lips twisted. 'And I suppose you think having a baby with a man makes everything else all right.'

'No——'

'Good. Because it doesn't. Oh, you might as well know, I only had Maria because I was afraid Alex might dump me. Why do you think the marriage has lasted this long? I can assure you, it wasn't because we've been working at it.'

Camilla didn't know what to say. 'But you must have loved the baby,' she ventured, and Virginia gave her an old-fashioned look.

'Must I? Cam, I'm not the maternal type. Maybe if she'd been a boy...' She moved her bony shoulders in a dismissive gesture. 'What does it matter? It's all hypothetical anyway. Grant says——'

'Grant!' Camilla's jaw dropped. 'Grant Blaisdell!' she echoed, and Virginia uttered a low groan.

'Oh, God, he really will kill me now,' she moaned, wrapping her arms about herself, and rocking backwards and forwards in her chair. 'Cam, you've got to promise me not to tell Alex about Grant. Please, if you care anything about me you won't mention his name.'

Camilla was staggered. 'You mean...he *is* involved in this?'

Virginia pressed her lips together. 'I can't answer that.'

'You just have.' Camilla rubbed the back of her neck disbelievingly. 'Grant Blaisdell,' she said again, moving her head from side to side. 'I don't believe it.'

Virginia shrugged. 'How else do you think I knew you were at the office? Grant told me. Oh—inadvertently, I think. But he told me just the same.'

'But Virginia, the man's a creep!'

'No, he's not.' Virginia was defensive now. 'You don't understand, Cam. Grant and I have known each other for years. He...he was the one who introduced me to Alex, actually. We knew one another in London. Before he came to work for the Conti Corporation.'

'You did?' Camilla's tongue circled her upper lip. 'Even so——'

'Even so nothing! He loves me, Cam. I know he does. And I love him. I do.'

Camilla studied Virginia's face, but it was difficult to read her expression through the veil. Nevertheless, there had been an element of self-delusion in her words, and Camilla wondered if Virginia was having second thoughts.

'You said *I* was the only person you could trust,' she reminded her now. 'Where does...Grant...come into all this?'

'Oh...' Virginia moved her head frustratedly. 'Well— if you must know, it was his idea.'

'Kidnapping your own daughter and disappearing, you mean?'

'It wasn't like that.'

'I'd say it was exactly like that,' retorted Camilla, and then, realising she was in danger of alienating the other woman, she tempered her tone. 'But what did you hope to achieve by it?'

'You wouldn't understand.' Virginia looked sulky now.

'Try me.'

'No. I...oh, it's all gone wrong, terribly wrong!'

Camilla's mouth went dry. 'Maria's all right, isn't she?' she asked. 'Nothing...nothing's happened to her?'

'No.' Virginia was indignant. 'What do you think I am? She is my daughter, too, poor little bitch.'

'So—what do you mean?' Camilla tried to be patient. 'What *has* gone wrong?'

'I don't know. I don't know.' Virginia's shoulders hunched, and she put one hand over her head in an unknowingly protective gesture. 'Cam—I want to trust him. I do. But . . . I'm not sure any more. I'm not sure of anything.'

Camilla hesitated. 'You're talking about . . . Grant?'

'Who else?' Virginia didn't seem to comprehend that she could have meant someone else. 'He said we'd be together. He said I wouldn't have to worry about . . . about anything. But he's changed, Cam. He's changed. I don't know what he's thinking any more.'

Camilla blinked. She had the feeling she was on the brink of learning everything, but, like a novice in a minefield, she didn't know where to proceed. Virginia's mood was so mercurial, so volatile. Any minute she might change her mind, and if Camilla said the wrong thing she might lose this chance forever.

'Virginia,' she said softly, 'you said you could trust me. So—why don't you? Tell me what you want me to do.'

Virginia sighed, and cast another nervous glance over her shoulder. Then, anchoring her trembling hands together again, she said, 'I want you to talk to Alex.'

'Me?' Camilla caught her breath.

'Yes, you.' Virginia nodded vigorously, the veil flapping about her cheeks like the wings of a bat. 'You've got to persuade him to do what Grant wants him to do. If not . . . if not . . .'

Camilla was horrified. 'You're afraid of him, Virginia!'

'No.' But the word belied the agitation she could not conceal. 'Cam, this is important to me. I need you to intercede on my behalf. If . . . if anything goes wrong——'

'What could go wrong?'

'Don't ask.' Virginia got up from the table. 'Believe me, you don't want to know,' she added harshly, and before Camilla could do anything to stop her she hurried away across the paved courtyard.

Camilla went to follow her, but the waitress appeared, and, realising she hadn't paid for her drink, she fumbled in her bag for some notes. Flinging them on to the table, she raced after Virginia, but the other woman had left the building, and when Camilla emerged into the sunlight there was no sign of the dark-clad figure.

She took a taxi back to Kumaru. She did consider returning to Alex's office, but the thought that she might encounter Grant Blaisdell made that a negative option. She had no wish to see him again, and even the knowledge that her instinctive dislike for him had not been misplaced did not make the thought of meeting him again any more acceptable. Indeed, she was half afraid that if she did see him the temptation to confront him with his involvement might have got the better of her. And, if fear of what he might do if he discovered she was deceiving him had added to Virginia's general air of edginess, Camilla had no right to betray her.

This time she had no difficulty in gaining access to the estate, though running the gauntlet of the avid newspeople did put a strain on her nervous system. She kept her head averted, one hand half covering her eyes, as the taxi driver drove between the peering faces, hoping the flashing cameras wouldn't capture her image on film.

Mama Lu met her at the door, and, judging by her expression, her return was not a moment too soon. 'Where've you been?' the housekeeper exclaimed, accompanying her into the coolness of the living-room. 'Alex has been on the phone every half-hour, wanting to know if you got back. Seems like you two can't be together but what you're spatting. D'you want to share with me what it was you had to tell him, now? Like a trouble shared, is a trouble halved—isn't that what they say?'

Camilla hesitated. It was probably unwise to discuss anything with Mama Lu, knowing, as she did, that whatever she said would get back to Alex one way or the other. But the urge to talk to someone who posed neither a threat nor a disaster was appealing, and as she toyed with the prospect the housekeeper took charge.

'You sit yourself down, and I'll go and get us some tea,' she announced, taking Camilla's silence for assent. 'Then we'll have a good old bitch, hmm? Like about men, and how they screw up our lives.'

She was gone before Camilla could either agree or disagree. Moving with the unexpected lightness of foot that was peculiar to her, she hurried away to prepare a tray, and Camilla sank down on to one of the squashy couches by the window. She felt too weary to offer much of an argument anyway, she decided. It had been a tiring day, and it wasn't over yet.

The tray Mama Lu set before her a few minutes later looked every bit as inviting as the meals she had enjoyed since she had come here. Or perhaps 'enjoyed' was not precisely the right word, she conceded. Mealtimes, particularly if Alex was present, had become something of an ordeal, and, although the food was delightful, she hadn't been able to appreciate it.

However, after not having any lunch, Camilla found she was hungry now. With Mama Lu's encouragement, she swallowed at least half a dozen smoked-salmon sandwiches and drank several cups of tea, finishing with a fluffy scone fairly oozing with cream and jam.

The housekeeper sat beside her, her generous bulk causing a corresponding dent in the soft leather. But she rationed herself to only one sandwich and one cup of tea, seemingly content to watch Camilla empty the plate.

She waited until Camilla was swallowing the last morsel of pastry, before saying gently, 'So . . . what happened? Was it to do with Mrs Virginia?'

'Was what to do with Virginia?' Camilla felt the guilty colour invade her cheeks as she spoke, and then, realising what Mama Lu was referring to, she recovered herself. 'Oh—you mean my reason for wanting to see Al—Mr Conti.' She paused to give herself time to get her breath back. 'Yes. Yes, it was. I—um—I remembered she had mentioned the fact . . . that . . . that I had been here three days. When . . . when she phoned, I mean.'

'Aha!' Mama Lu inclined her head. 'And?'

'Someone must have told her,' explained Camilla quickly. 'Someone else. I . . . thought at first it must have

been a member of the staff here. Or...or one of the
security people.'

'I see.' The housekeeper nodded. 'But not now, hmm?'

'Not now what?' Camilla was confused.

'You said you thought *at first* it might be someone
here. But now you've changed your mind. Why's that?'

'Well...' Camilla's face felt hotter than ever. 'I mean—
who would do it? I'm sure all the staff are...are
trustworthy.'

'I'd say so,' agreed Mama Lu, shrugging her plump
shoulders. 'So what did Alex say?'

'Alex? Oh, you mean Mr Conti.' Camilla used every
opportunity to gain herself some time. 'Well—he had
already worked that out, I think.'

'And that's why he was mad?'

'He wasn't mad.' Camilla put up a nervous hand to
her hair. The knot she had secured that morning was
still intact, though somewhat the worse for wear, judging
by the damp strands that trailed down her neck. 'Gosh,
it's hot, isn't it? Even with the air-conditioning.'

Mama Lu lifted her shoulders. 'It depends what you've
been doing, doesn't it?'

Camilla sighed. She was tempted to ask Mama Lu
what she thought she had been doing, but fear of what
the other woman might say held her back. Instead, she
picked up her bag and smoothed the shiny leather,
allowing the silence to stretch before making her excuses
and leaving.

'So who does Alex think told her you were here?'

Evidently Mama Lu couldn't read her mind, Camilla
decided with some relief. But her question needed an
answer, and she made a helpless gesture. 'I don't know.'

'Who do you think it was?'

'Me?' Camilla couldn't look the woman in the eyes,
but she darted a swift glance at her. 'It...it could be
anyone,' she stammered, wishing she were not such a
poor liar. 'Someone...someone in the office perhaps.
Lots of people work there.'

'Like Mr Grant maybe?'

'Mr Grant?' But Mama Lu was too perceptive, and
Camilla was finding it increasingly difficult to hide her
reaction. 'As...as I say, I don't know, do I?' she de-

clared, wishing she had never started this. 'I—er—I think I'll go and take a shower. Walking round town has made me sticky.'

She got up stiffly, but Mama Lu levered her bulk off the sofa to block her exit. 'You want some advice?'

'Some advice?' Camilla tried to look condescending, and failed. 'I don't think I——'

'You got something to tell Alex—anything at all—you tell him. Don't wait for him to find out for himself. Not unless you think you can handle the fall-out, that is.'

Camilla swallowed. 'Mama Lu, this is ridiculous——'

'Is it?' Mama Lu didn't look as if she thought it was. 'You been missing for the best part of three hours!'

'I went shopping.'

'What'd you buy?'

Camilla gasped. 'I don't have to answer that.' She took a deep breath, and then, rather recklessly, she challenged, 'Where do you think I've been? Having lunch with Virginia, perhaps?'

Camilla sat on her balcony, watching the shadows deepen over the terrace below. It might be the last chance she had to enjoy the reflected rays of the sun, turning the sky to molten gold on the eastern horizon, and she tried to enjoy the exotic spectacle. The sea was changing colour, too, the blue paling to smoothest silver, shining opaquely, where the earth and sky combined.

The air was delicious, warm, and subtly scented, yet cool against her skin. She could probably feel its coolness because her body was so hot, she thought uneasily. Not even an ice-cold shower could temper her emotions.

Yet when she thought of confronting Alex she did feel a sense of chill. Perhaps not physically, but certainly mentally, her brain in a turmoil as she struggled to come to terms with what she must do. Mama Lu was right: she had to tell Alex that she had seen Virginia. But why she hadn't told him immediately was something he was bound to want an answer to, and she didn't have one.

Not that Mama Lu knew she had seen Virginia, of course. In spite of appearing to know what Camilla had been doing, even the housekeeper had backed down in the face of Camilla's defiance. She might suspect that her absence had not been entirely innocent, but even she didn't believe that Virginia might have come out of hiding to find her.

Which left Camilla in the invidious position of either keeping her meeting with Virginia a secret—an option she couldn't honestly justify, if she cared anything for the child's safety; or she could tell Alex what had happened—and risk his suspecting that she had known all about the meeting before she had insisted on being brought into Honolulu.

Of course, there was one other alternative. She could just take the next plane out of here—in any direction—and leave the Contis to sort out their own troubles. After all, now that Virginia had told her that Grant Blaisdell was involved it would be difficult to tell Alex anything without implicating his cousin. And how could she do that? She had no proof. And there was always the possibility that Virginia might be lying. She'd done it before, heaven knew!

She glanced at her watch. It was half-past six, and Alex wasn't home yet. She wondered if he was intending to spend another night in town. He could be. After what had happened between them that morning, it wouldn't surprise her if he took up permanent residence at his parents' house. And what was she going to do if he did? Wait until tomorrow before making any decision either way?

The sound of a car broke into her thoughts. She could hear the crunching of its tyres on the gravel, and the low hum of its engine. It had to be Alex, she thought, her mouth drying. Dear God, what was she going to do? Time was running out.

She couldn't sit on her balcony any longer. She couldn't go on pretending there was any escape from what she had to do. Virginia might be Maria's mother, but she was in no fit state to look after her at present. Alex had to be told she had seen her. He had to know what Virginia had asked her to do.

She was standing in front of the dressing-table, applying a cooling moisturiser to her cheeks, when there was a knock at her door. Her hands were already shaking as they smoothed the cream on to her skin, and the heavy-handed summons almost made her drop the jar.

'Yes,' she called, deciding the navy blue teddy was every bit as decent as the bikini she had worn the day before. 'Come... come in, Mama Lu. Does... does Mr Conti want to see me?'

'Yes. He does,' declared Alex as the door was thrust open and he stepped into the room. His eyes raked her startled figure, darkening as they rested on the high breasts and slim hips outlined by the silk undergarment. Then he lifted his shoulders, as if justifying his intrusion. 'D'you want to put on a robe?' he suggested. 'I've got something to tell you.'

CHAPTER TWELVE

CAMILLA snatched up the white bathrobe she had worn after her shower, her face a scarlet beacon above the terry towelling. Alex was the last person she had expected to walk into her room, and combined with her embarrassment was a not unnatural feeling of resentment that he should think he could barge into her apartments without even announcing his intentions.

The bathrobe was damp, and it clung unpleasantly to her skin. But, short of asking him to leave until she had put on some clothes, she didn't have an alternative. Besides, his expression didn't encourage her to attempt to avoid this encounter.

'Something to tell me?' she ventured at last, hoping her voice didn't sound as anxious to his ears as it did to her own. 'About...about Virginia?'

'What else?'

Alex closed the door, and the sound it made as he did so echoed ominously round the room. It reminded Camilla of her own vulnerability where this man was concerned; reminded her that she had fewer friends on the island than Virginia did herself.

Alex was still wearing his business suit, but now he thrust his hands into his trouser pockets, spreading the jacket wide and drawing the cloth taut across his muscled thighs. Camilla found herself wondering if his legs were as darkly tanned as the parts of his body she could see, and quickly stifled the thought. For God's sake, this was not the time to entertain such trivialities, she told herself. She must concentrate on what was important. Virginia's whereabouts for starters.

For all the aggressive way he had entered her room, Alex now seemed in no hurry to get to the point. On the contrary, much to Camilla's discomfort, he ap-

peared quite content to assess her reactions to him, and
she was sure he had sensed her instinctive unease.

Then, as if growing tired of the game, he pulled an
envelope out of his pocket, and tapped it against his
palm. 'Do you know what this is?'

Camilla frowned. 'No.'

'No?'

'Well, it looks like a letter,' she volunteered defensively. 'Is...is it from Virginia?'

'Don't you know?'

'No.'

Alex looked down at the letter, then up at her, his
dark eyes narrowed and intent. 'You've never seen this
envelope before?'

'No.' Camilla swallowed. 'Is it from Virginia? For
heaven's sake, what does it say?'

Alex hesitated. Then he tossed the envelope on to the
dressing-table beside her. 'Read it,' he said abruptly. 'It's
typewritten, but the signature's Virginia's.'

Camilla ignored the letter. 'I...I'd rather you told me
what's in it,' she said, unwilling to reveal how her hands
were shaking. She was already under suspicion apparently. He wouldn't understand that her nervousness came
as much from an awareness of him as from any threat
the letter might hold.

Alex stared at her for a long minute, and then he came
to pick up the letter again, flicking open the envelope
and extracting the single sheet of paper it contained. 'You
were right,' he said as Camilla stared at him uncompre-
hendingly. 'Virginia does want a divorce. If I want to
see Maria again I have to agree to her terms.'

Camilla hadn't been aware of holding her breath until
the air rushed out of her lungs with a noisy whoosh.
But the freedom of knowing exactly what Virginia did
want was such a relief, and she couldn't understand why
Alex still looked so strange.

'Well,' she said, smoothing the palms of her hands
down the sides of the bathrobe, 'that's good news, isn't
it? I mean—now that you know what she wants you can
make a deal.'

'Can I?' Alex regarded her speculatively, and she realised that by making him come and pick up the letter

she had inadvertently narrowed the space between them.
'I notice you don't ask what she wants. Is that because
you already know?'

'Me?' Camilla was staggered. 'How could I know?'
But her colour was still high, and she was sure he didn't
believe her.

'Do you know how I got this letter?' Alex enquired
smoothly, and she moved her head in a jerky negative
motion. 'It was handed to the receptionist in the Conti
building. By a child. A child who said the letter had
been given to him by a lady.'

Camilla tried to sound offhand. 'So?'

'So...the woman who handed him the letter could
have been you.'

Camilla gasped. 'That's ridiculous!'

'Is it?' Alex was studying her expressive face with raw
intensity. 'If I add to that the fact that the woman was
also wearing a *black veil*, will you see my dilemma?'

Camilla took a deep breath. 'Why would I wear a...a
black veil?'

Alex moved then. With a speed that left her no time
to offer any resistance, he lunged towards her, gripping
her shoulders and forcing her to look at herself in the
mirror. 'Now, do I have to give you a reason?' he snarled,
as her hair, still loose from her shower, spilled its
brilliance about her shoulders. 'Why else would anyone
want to wear a veil to hide their face from a *stranger*?'
he demanded contemptuously. 'Unless they were afraid
even a child would remember such a distinctive
characteristic!'

'No. No, it wasn't me!' Camilla moved her head from
side to side, unaware that, as she did so, its silky texture
was caressing his face. Her paramount concern was to
make him believe her, and there was no longer any doubt
in her mind about what she had to do. 'It wasn't me,'
she repeated, her voice barely audible. 'I had nothing to
do with it. If...if you'll let me go I'll tell you...'

But Alex wasn't listening to her. In reaching for her
as he had, in grabbing her shoulders and forcing her to
look in the mirror, the hastily tied belt of the bathrobe
had loosened. As she had struggled to protest her inno-

cence, the two sides of the robe had fallen free, exposing the seductive teddy, and the delicate skin beneath.

Her stomach quivered as she realised how the reflection of her body had distracted him. The trembling muscles were almost concave as she stiffened in his grasp. But the action only served to heighten the upward thrust of her breasts, and the creamy skin swelled enticingly above the lacy trim of the basque.

'Alex——' she choked, but her use of his name fell on deaf ears. And it was hardly a denial when she was making no effort to free herself from his bruising grasp. On the contrary, when his blazing eyes moved down over the lissom curves of her body they ignited a flame inside her that carried to every shuddering extremity.

She knew she should have dragged the folds of the bathrobe about her, but she didn't. She knew she should have pulled away from him, but she didn't do that either. And when the hands on her arms lifted to hook the robe off her shoulders, and allowed it to fall in a heap about her ankles, she knew it was too late to think about resisting him.

Even so, she was not prepared for the deluge of feeling that gripped her when his hands slid from her shoulders to the rigid curve of her ribcage. His thumbs only brushed the undersides of her breasts as they moved down over the sensitive narrowing at her waist, to the proud swell of her hips, but everywhere he touched the skin responded alarmingly. Indeed, it took an actual physical effort to prevent herself from covering his hands with her own, and when they spread against her palpitating stomach she shook uncontrollably.

'So soft,' he breathed, and the draught of air against her throat brought her eyes up to his. While her gaze had been riveted by the downward sweep of his hands he had bent his head, and now his tongue moved sensuously against her neck.

But his eyes held hers, and, realising this was her last chance to try to appeal to his conscience, if not her own, she took a trembling breath. 'We...we...can't,' she got out unsteadily, but Alex was indifferent to her pleas.

'Why not?' he demanded, his teeth nipping the tender flesh and leaving reddened circles against her skin. 'Don't pretend you don't want it just as much as I do.'

'That...that's not the point...' she stammered, but he didn't let her go.

'On the contrary,' he contradicted harshly, 'it's the only point to any of this,' and, twisting her round in his arms, he brought his mouth to hers.

Camilla's senses swam at the first touch of his lips. She had hung on to a faint hope that she might be able to control the extent of her response to him, but she was wrong. The hungry pressure of his mouth was too demanding, the hot invasion of his tongue too mind-bending to allow any kind of coherent thought to dominate. She was on fire for him, kissing him back with a raw abandon that had nothing to do with intelligent reasoning. She wanted him. Dear God, he was right: she *wanted* him! And, no matter how she might deny it to herself, that had never happened before.

Her whole body was suffused with the pleasure his mouth was exacting. Little rivulets of flame sped along her veins, melting her bones and thickening her blood. His tongue seduced hers, assaulted hers, sucked hers into his mouth with a greedy possession, and her arms crept around him without her really being aware of it.

Her breasts were taut and swollen, straining against the restrictions of the teddy, and desperate to be free. When Alex's mouth left hers to seek the delicate skin that rose above the silk she tried to communicate this to him, and when he tipped the straps off her shoulders, and pressed the bodice down to her waist, she sighed with satisfaction. She trembled, too, when his mouth took possession of one engorged peak and suckled eagerly. She had never experienced the surge of emotion the sight of his dark head against her breast inspired in her. Her hand moved to cradle his head, her fingers sliding into his dark hair, and when his hands gripped her hips, she arched convulsively against him.

Alex caught his breath as the pliant contours of her body moulded themselves to his. One long leg had coiled itself around his, and, taking advantage of her yielding weakness, he cupped his hands beneath her bottom, and carried her to the bed. Camilla tumbled back on to the cool counterpane without protest. Her fingers assisted his as he tore off his shirt and jacket before coming down on top of her.

His mouth sought hers again, more urgently now, and she felt his hands peeling the clinging teddy from her hips. Her moist limbs, freed now from any restraint, wound themselves about him, and Alex's groan of satisfaction was buried in her hair.

His hands moved lower, sliding between her legs to find the slick curls that hid the eager core of her womanhood. The muscles there jerked and constricted beneath his probing caress, and Camilla moaned, deep in her throat, as he stroked the palpitating source.

But he was still half dressed, and when his mouth laved a heated trail to her navel she uttered a choking protest. 'Please,' she breathed, shifting urgently beneath his caress. Her hands sought the buckle of his belt, and he rolled on to his side to enable her to loosen it. But the rigid swelling beneath the cloth was what intrigued her most, and her fingers moved to encircle his hardness, drawing down his zip, and taking him into her hands.

'Oh, God!' he muttered, tearing open the buckle himself, and disposing of the button beneath. 'Camilla, I have to do it now! I have to be inside you. You're driving me insane...'

Later Camilla was to wonder what would have happened if Alex had actually been caught in the act of love when Mama Lu knocked at the door. She doubted he would have recovered so quickly from that eventuality as he did from only being on the brink. As it was, she could have screamed with frustration when the throbbing heat of his arousal was withdrawn. Seconds before, it had felt like hot velvet against her thigh, a swollen, pulsatingly hard tumescence that would satisfy the burning ache inside her. But, by the time Camilla had regained her senses sufficiently to understand that there was someone knocking at her door, Alex was thrusting the tail of his shirt into the waistband of his trousers.

'Put this on,' he said, picking the bathrobe off the floor and tossing it to her. And, although his words were innocent of censure, there was a savage denigration in his eyes.

Camilla felt dizzy as she got off the bed and did as he had ordered. Too much emotion, and too swift a transition to reality, had made her doubt her own identity, and she blinked a little dazedly as Alex knotted his tie.

She was still struggling to tie the cord of the robe when Alex went to open the door, and he frowned disapprovingly. It seemed obvious he blamed her for what had happened, and, as sanity reasserted itself, Camilla also blamed herself. Dear God, she thought, trying to smooth the hair which only minutes before Alex had disordered; she had almost committed an unforgivable sin! While everyone else was desperate for news of Virginia and Maria, she had seduced—and been seduced by purely selfish emotions. For the last fifteen minutes she hadn't given a thought to anyone or anything but Alex, and even now, with the knowledge of hindsight, her body was still clamouring for a satisfaction it hadn't received.

She dreaded Mama Lu's coming in. She dreaded the housekeeper looking at her, and guessing what had been going on. There was no way Camilla could face her without revealing how she felt. She didn't have the kind of character that could hide its innermost feelings.

But, as it happened, she didn't have to. Within a minute of Mama Lu's knocking at the door, Alex was opening it and letting himself out. 'Miss Richards isn't very well, so I've suggested she get some rest,' Camilla heard him say as he closed the door firmly behind him. 'She's got a headache, and I was in the bathroom, getting her a drink, when you knocked at the door. That was why I didn't hear...'

The sound of his voice died away as he and the housekeeper walked back along the corridor, and Camilla slumped on to the edge of the bed. Whatever Mama Lu might really think, she was evidently not prepared to go against her employer's instructions, and whatever she had wanted to say could apparently wait until later.

Camilla sighed, wiping her damp forehead with the back of her hand. Now that Alex was gone it was becoming increasingly difficult to believe what had ac-

tually happened, but the sight of the envelope, lying on
the floor where he had dropped it, reminded her sharply
of his reasons for coming.

Reminded her, too, that she had said nothing to Alex
about seeing Virginia. The arrival of the letter, obviously given to the child to deliver by Virginia herself,
had superceded everything else. And then, when Alex
had touched her...

She swallowed unevenly. She still didn't know what
terms Virginia—and Grant—had stated in the letter, but
nothing would persuade her to read it. Getting off the
bed, she picked up the envelope, pushed the letter inside,
and stuffed it into a drawer. However unwilling Alex
might be to talk to her again, sooner or later he would
come back for the letter. And then she would tell him
what Virginia had said, whether or not he chose to believe she had had no part in the meeting.

Camilla slept fitfully. She had awakened several times,
convinced it must be morning, only to find it was still
the early hours. She had wished she had something she
could take to relax her. A sleeping pill, perhaps, or even
a warm drink, but she didn't. And the idea of leaving
her room to go in search of Mama Lu's kitchen was not
appealing.

Besides it might be difficult to explain why she was
wandering around the house in the middle of the night.
She was sure Mama Lu already suspected something of
what had happened the evening before. When she'd
brought Camilla's supper—to her room, in keeping with
Alex's assertion that she had had a headache—she had
viewed the younger woman's flushed features with some
speculation. Even though Camilla had got into bed, and
was feigning feeling unwell, the housekeeper hadn't
seemed convinced. And if she found her erstwhile patient
padding the halls of the house, ostensibly in search of
a nightcap, she might suspect her motives were not as
innocent as they seemed.

Camilla knew she couldn't do that to Alex, however
she might feel. He had enough to worry about as it was,
without having to defend himself to the housekeeper. In
any case, Camilla had no wish to draw any more at-

tention to herself. Her best plan would be to tell Alex all she knew in the morning, and then make definite arrangements for leaving.

She was up at first light, and down on the terrace for breakfast before Mama Lu had even laid the table. In a coffee-coloured silk shirt and matching trousers, she felt more capable to face whatever was before her, and not even the housekeeper was going to distract her mood. She had even confined her hair in an uncompromising plait, with no beguiling strands to soften her taut profile.

But it wasn't Mama Lu who came to set the table. It was Wong Lee, his olive-skinned features as taut as Camilla's own. There was no cheerful smile to split his lips; they were tightly pressed together this morning, and there was no teasing conversation to make her feel relaxed.

'Um...is...isn't Mr Conti joining me for breakfast?' Camilla ventured when the man laid only one set of cutlery on the cloth, and Wong Lee shook his head.

'No, Miss Richards,' he replied, folding his hands and shaking his head. 'The *padrone*...he left for town some hours ago.'

'Some hours ago!' Camilla was disturbed. 'But—it's only seven o'clock now!'

'Yes.' Wong Lee bowed over his hands. 'I will get you some coffee, Miss Richards,' he added, without any further explanation. 'Then you can tell me how you would like your eggs, yes?'

'No. That is...' Camilla put out a hand as he would have jogged away. 'Is that all you can tell me? That Mr Conti's gone into town? Why did he go into town? Has there been some development?'

'There was a letter, Miss Richards,' replied Wong Lee reluctantly, and Camilla gave an impatient sigh.

'Yes. Yes, I know that!' she exclaimed. And then, realising she could hardly blame him for the situation, she lowered her voice. 'But I still don't understand. Why would...why would he—Mr Conti—go into town in the middle of the night?' She paused. 'Did he get another message? Do you know what's going on?'

'No, Miss Richards.'

Wong Lee's sibilant lisp was polite, but negative. Bowing again, he left her, and Camilla had the distinct impression that if he did know anything he wasn't going to confide in her. And he must know something, she thought uneasily. He and Mama Lu both.

But when Wong Lee came back with the coffee she didn't press him. It wasn't fair to involve him in her problems, and she was possibly jumping to the wrong conclusions anyway. Maybe, like her, Alex hadn't been able to sleep. But, unlike her, he had not been confined to his apartments.

Refusing anything but orange juice and some toast, Camilla breakfasted alone. It was another beautiful morning, and she wondered how anyone living in these surroundings could still want more. Virginia had had everything, she thought: a handsome husband, a beautiful home, a loving family; what was it that had caused her to waste her life? She had had more than one chance to start again. But something—or someone—had driven her onward. Grant Blaisdell? Camilla pondered. Or simply a fatal flaw in her own make-up?

She was getting up from her chair when she heard the car. Alex, she thought weakly, not really prepared for this meeting. She had been prepared when she came down to breakfast. But Wong Lee's words, and the lapse of time, had robbed her of the advantage.

Nevertheless, she had to see him, and, deciding she would rather speak to him in private, she walked through the garden-room, and up the twisting staircase to the landing. At least the polished floors would give some warning if Mama Lu chose to join them, she thought. She had no intention of embarrassing herself again.

But the man who was standing in the arching entrance hall was not Alex. It was Grant Blaisdell, and Camilla's initial impulse was to turn and flee. He was the last person she had expected to come to Alex's house, and only the knowledge that he couldn't know about her meeting with Virginia kept her from showing her feelings.

'Hi,' he said, and he looked and spoke so normally that Camilla could only marvel at his duplicity. How dared he come here, she wondered, acting as if nothing

had happened when, at the very least, he was culpable
of aiding Virginia's disappearance?

But she mustn't let him know she doubted his sincerity. And not just for Virginia's sake, either. Until she
had spoken to Alex, until she had at least *tried* to warn
him of Grant's conspiracy, she was the only person, besides Virginia, who knew of his involvement. And if
Virginia was apprehensive of his motives, shouldn't she
be, too?

'Hi,' she responded now, making sure her voice revealed none of the anxiety she was feeling. 'Did...did
you want to see...Alex?'

'*Alex?*' Grant gave her a mocking look. 'What happened to "Mr Conti"'?'

'All right. Mr Conti, then.' Camilla was in no mood
to play word-games, but she tempered her response with
a tight smile. 'Anyway, if you have come to see him,
he's not here——'

'I know.'

'You know?' Camilla's surprise was genuine. 'Oh, but
I——'

'That's why I'm here,' explained Grant swiftly. 'It's
good news, Camilla. Virginia's been found.'

'She has?'

Camilla could only stare at him, dumbfounded, and
Grant nodded. 'Yes. Isn't it marvellous? Alex called to
tell me, and I thought you might like to come with me.
Virginia's been taken to hospital, and I'm sure he'd
welcome your help with Maria.'

CHAPTER THIRTEEN

CAMILLA had never been on a yacht before. Occasionally she had wondered if she would make a good sailor, but the opportunity to find out had never arisen, and it had not been an omission that had troubled her greatly. It was one of those things she had expected to face if it ever happened, and never in her wildest dreams had she imagined that one day she might learn to hate the slapping sound of water against pressed steel, and the uneven rise and fall of the deck beneath her.

But then, she had never anticipated that anyone might ever take her prisoner, or that they might choose for her prison the stifling engine-room of Alex's yacht. Of all the many luxurious apartments on the yacht where she might have been confined, she had been thrust into the engine-room, and the smell of oil and diesel was nauseating.

To say she was frightened would have been an understatement. She was terrified, not least because she now knew what Grant was capable of. He would do anything to achieve his own ends, she realised, even to the extent of disposing of her if he had no other option.

Of course, when she had accompanied him to Honolulu she had had no idea that it might be a trap. How could she have? Her excitement at hearing that Virginia and Maria were free had superceded all else, and, despite what Virginia had told her, it would have been difficult to refuse to go with him.

Besides, he had told Mama Lu the same story. The housekeeper had wept tears of joy when she'd heard that Alex's daughter was safe and well. So far as Virginia was concerned, her relief had been visibly less enthusiastic, but they had all been excited that their fears had been unjustified.

Except Grant, Camilla acknowledged despairingly. If Virginia had been found—and she had only his word that she had—Grant must know his position was in jeopardy. But Virginia was an addict. It was a well-known fact that she had been an addict for years, and Alex already knew her for a liar. It was possible that if she maintained that Grant had been her accomplice—and Grant himself might deter her from making any uncorroborated accusations—no one would believe her. But Camilla was another matter. Camilla had spoken to Virginia when she had been under no pressure to defend herself, and Virginia had told Camilla of Grant's involvement. Camilla would be believed, and Grant knew that.

If only she had told Alex what had happened, Camilla thought bitterly. If only passion hadn't overwhelmed reason, and she had alerted him to what Virginia had said. But events had overtaken her, and this morning he had been gone.

This morning? Camilla wondered. It was impossible to judge what time it was, or indeed if it was even the same day. Light did filter into the engine-room around the frame of the door, but, as she had been unconscious, she couldn't honestly be sure what day it was.

Camilla groaned as the painful pressure of the ropes that bound her wrists to her ankles cut into her flesh. If only she had insisted on ringing Alex before delivering herself into Grant's hands, she thought now. But how could she have done that without arousing Grant's suspicions? And at that time she had still believed he knew nothing about her meeting with Virginia.

And he had behaved so convincingly, she remembered, recalling the journey into Honolulu with a shiver. He had sounded so convincing, in fact, that she had actually wondered if Virginia had lied to her. But that had just been part of his strategy, and she should have trusted her initial instincts about him and been on her guard.

Honolulu had been quiet, she remembered, with just the street-cleaners and a few intrepid joggers occupying Kalakaua Avenue. There had been cars about, of course, and taxis, but she had hardly noticed them anyway, so intent had she been on reaching their destination.

She supposed she should have been more wary, but the very fact that he had brought her into Honolulu had convinced her of his sincerity. If she had entertained any doubts—and, in all honesty, Camilla couldn't remember doing so—she would have expected him to make his move when they were out of town. But Grant was cleverer than that. He hadn't wanted any witnesses to what he planned to do, and she had been so gullible that it had been comparatively easy for him.

Nevertheless, she had looked doubtful when Grant had turned off the main thoroughfare and approached the yacht marina. But his casual explanation that Virginia and Maria had been hiding out on Alex's yacht had sounded so believable that Camilla hadn't argued. After all, it was common knowledge that the best hiding-places were the most obvious ones. And Alex would never have expected Virginia to stay so close to home.

That was why Camilla had accompanied him on board the yacht in good faith. The place had looked deserted, but, knowing Alex's desire to keep this affair quiet, she hadn't been alarmed. Why should she expect to see a police car, when the police hadn't been informed of Virginia's disappearance? So far as they—and the Press—were concerned, Virginia had left of her own free will. Unless Alex asked for their assistance, they wouldn't interfere.

The yacht was huge, a floating palace of a boat with every conceivable luxury appliance. It was exactly the kind of place Virginia would choose to use as a hide-out, thought Camilla wryly. It was private, and comfortable, with every modern convenience.

Including a telephone, Camilla noticed at once, as they entered the enormous state-room. Not that she was looking for such things. She was more concerned with the prospect of seeing Alex again, after what had happened the night before. And with meeting his daughter, the child who might still have the ability to repair her parents' relationship.

However, the state-room was empty, and, although she felt the first pricklings of unease, Camilla realised that someone hiding out would hardly advertise their presence so blatantly. Consequently, she followed Grant

into the much smaller cabin aft, where the evidence of
a prolonged occupation was unmistakable: empty fast-
food packages and magazines were strewn everywhere,
and the unpleasant smell of stale food permeated the
atmosphere. There were dirty cups and glasses, too,
making permanent stains on the teak-wood fittings, and,
more chillingly, a syringe, tossed carelessly on to the
floor.

But this room was empty, too, and the sight of another
of the dolls Camilla had seen at the house, lying forgotten on the floor, reminded her of why she was here.
Where was Maria? And, more significantly, where was
Alex?

Looking back now, Camilla realised she had been off
guard. But seeing the room where Virginia had hidden
herself and her daughter away, imagining what it must
have been like for a little girl, confined to one room when
she was used to living at Kumaru, had blinded her to
any fears for her own safety. She realised she had still
believed that Alex would appear at any moment, and
when she had turned to Grant she had had no other
thought in her mind.

And that was where she had made her mistake—well,
the last of many, she conceded wearily. But the trouble
was, in spite of everything that had happened, she still
had an inherent belief that there must have been some
mistake, that Grant would not have been involved. Even
the abandoned syringe had been no more than proof of
Virginia's instability, and when she saw the syringe in
Grant's hand it was too late to do anything about it. Her
reflexes were not swift enough to avoid the jabbing
needle, and the pain of its unguarded entry into her arm
was agonising.

She had tried to scream, but Grant had been prepared
for that, and, although she had attempted to bite the
fingers he crushed across her mouth, already the drug
was weakening her defences.

'What...what have you done?' she remembered
gasping, as her arm, and progressively the rest of her
body, began to lose feeling, and Grant stuffed a dirty
napkin into her mouth to keep her silent.

'Don't worry,' he said harshly, 'you're not dying. Not yet, anyway. It's just a simple tranquilliser. Just to make you...co-operative, shall we say?'

Camilla's tongue felt swollen. The linen napkin was filling her mouth, and she was sure she was choking. But there was nothing she could do about it. The insidious effects of the drug were numbing all her muscles, and, long before he had finished tying her wrists, she had lost consciousness...

She had awakened to find herself locked in this airless prison. Her wrists were bound to her ankles, and she had been left squatting on the floor of the cabin, her knees drawn up to her chin. It was not a comfortable position, but that was the least of her worries. She had probably been left this way because Grant would know that her cramped legs would prevent her making any attempt to escape when he came to release her. *If* he came to release her, she reminded herself unsteadily. She had no reason to be sure that he would. But she refused to think of that.

Her mouth was so dry, and she wondered again how long it had been since breakfast. Judging from the desperate need she had to use the bathroom, she guessed it was only hours, and not days. But if she was left here overnight what would she do? The alternatives were too disgusting to contemplate, and once again her thoughts turned to calculating how long she could survive in this heat without food or water. Well, water, anyway, she amended stoically. Surely, if Grant didn't mean to kill her, he would have to come back, and soon?

At least the choking napkin had been removed. No doubt, once she had lost consciousness, Grant had felt able to allow her that small advantage. However, her lips were now sealed by a broad strip of plaster, so the possibility of her shouting for help had also been denied her.

Her head ached, no doubt from the after-effects of whatever substance he had used to render her unconscious. But at least her mind was clear. He could have given her heroin or morphine, drugs which, if taken in excess, could scramble your brain at the very least. Maybe he was saving that for later, she thought despairingly. Was it really conceivable to think that he would let her go?

But where was Virginia? In all of this, she was the only hope Camilla had. If she had been found, where was she? Was she really in the hospital as Grant had said?

She had no way of finding out. None whatsoever. She didn't even know if Virginia was still alive. 'In hospital' could mean anything. They had mortuaries in hospitals, didn't they? What if Virginia and Maria were both dead? What if she was the only person left who could connect Grant with Virginia's disappearance?

Panic was a potent incentive, and Camilla's need to use the bathroom became almost uncontrollable. Dear God, she thought, had she travelled all the way to Hawaii just to die, tied up in some grotty engine-room? Was this to be her punishment for falling in love with Virginia's husband? For she was in love with him; she couldn't deny that. Even if it damned her soul for all eternity.

But the thought of Alex reassured her. Alex wasn't a fool. Not like her. He wasn't gullible. Hadn't he monitored the call Virginia had made to her? Hadn't he been suspicious of that letter? If she disappeared, he wouldn't just abandon her. He'd want to know where she had gone, not least because he didn't trust her.

She groaned. But if Virginia and Maria had been found—dead or alive—he was unlikely to come here for some time. He might not even know where they had been living—or care! So long as they had been found, he would have far more important things to do.

She had cried earlier, hot aching tears that had left her with bleary eyes and a permanent sniff, but now she felt the cowardly wetness on her cheeks once again. It was no good, she defended herself. She wasn't the stuff of which heroines were made. She was just an ordinary woman caught up in extraordinary events—and she was afraid.

Gradually, the narrow slivers of light around the door disappeared. It was getting dark, she realised, shivering as the perspiration dried on her body and left her feeling chilled. But at least the air was distinctly fresher, and

although her whole body was aching she could breathe
a little easier.

But in the darkness she became prey to other fears,
and the sounds of contracting metal assumed other
guises. Were there rats on board? she wondered
anxiously, convinced she could see beady eyes staring at
her in the gloom. Was that a spider trailing its long legs
across the back of her neck? From sagging with weari-
ness, she came alert to every tiny movement in the cabin,
and only the plaster across her mouth prevented her from
screaming out loud. Eventually, however, exhaustion
overtook her. She was so tired, and, almost without her
realising it, her head tipped back against the hull, and
she slept.

The rocking of the yacht woke Camilla to the awareness
that it was daylight. She opened her eyes, sticky with
the salt of her tears, to find that her prison was dimly
illuminated again. Amazingly, she had survived the night
unscathed, and only the biting pull of the ropes, and
her own physical needs, remained to torment her.

But the feeling of relief she experienced didn't last
long. The realisation of what had disturbed her was
reinforced by the continued movement of the vessel, and
she panicked again as its implications dawned on her:
someone was on board the boat. Someone was walking
across the deck above her. Grant must have come back,
and in no time at all she was drenched with sweat.

However, he wasn't alone. Straining her ears, she was
sure she could hear voices, and her heart faltered at the
thought that he might have brought an accomplice with
him. Against Grant she had little chance. Against him
and someone else she was helpless.

Tears gathered in her eyes again, but she fought them
back. God, was she a total coward? she chided herself
disgustedly. Tears would achieve nothing with a man like
him, only prove what a weakling she was. Did she want
Grant Blaisdell to think he had broken her spirit? Even
if he had, he shouldn't have the satisfaction of knowing.

With her hands clenched over her knees, she waited
for them to come down to the engine-room. By her reck-
oning, it should take no more than a couple of minutes

to reach her. Two minutes in which she had to steel herself to face an uncertain future.

But nothing happened. No one came near the engine-room. And as she sat there, rigid with fear, she realised that one of the voices she could hear was feminine; and not only feminine, but a little girl's. *A little girl's!* Bewilderment gripped her. Who else could it be but Maria? But what was she doing here? Why had she come back? And, more significantly, who was with her?

She concentrated on the voices, on their whereabouts. One was definitely a man's, and she tried to identify it. Was it Alex? Could it be? It sounded like Alex to her aching ears. But was she just hallucinating? Superimposing what she wanted to hear on to what she could?

The voices were closer now, but her knowledge of the yacht was so minimal that she could only guess where they might be. She had been unconscious when Grant had stowed her in the engine-room. She didn't know where it was in relation to the other cabins. Was she fore or aft? A bitter smile tugged at her sealed lips, at her brain's acquisition of the correct nautical terms. What did she know about a yacht's specifications? she thought wretchedly. She just knew she was trapped, unable to reveal her whereabouts, unable even to open her mouth.

She closed her eyes against the awful hopelessness of her position. It was ironic—or, in her case, rather more than that—that Grant was the only person who knew where she was. If something had happened to him, if he had been forced to flee, what would happen to her then? His plans for her might not have been pleasant, but at least they would have been swift. If she was left to die here by degrees, dehydrating in the heat, it could take days.

The horror of this scenario filled her with despair. It couldn't be happening, she thought. It must all be a dream—like the dream she had had that Alex loved her. But when she opened her eyes the gloomy walls of her cell were still around her, and the sob that rose inside her burst out in a keening groan.

And then she heard the footsteps, the pattering sound of a child's shoe, and the more hesitant tread of a man's.

'It must have been a cat,' Camilla heard Alex say, practically outside the door, and for a moment she was too shocked to move.

'It didn't sound like a cat, Daddy,' a doubtful feminine voice answered him, and Camilla thought she had never heard anything so sweet. 'What's in here?' Maria added, and rattled the handle of the engine-room door.

'It's just where the diesels are housed,' Alex replied, and Camilla could imagine him taking his daughter's hand and drawing her away.

She went wild then, somehow managing to move her feet, and scrape them against the floor. At the same time she made a series of grunting noises through her nose, and when Alex opened the door she practically tumbled at his feet.

'God!'

Alex stared down at her in horror, and she had a moment to register the lines of strain that etched his cheeks. And then Maria, a small dark miniature of her paternal grandmother, squatted down beside her, and touched the plaster that covered her mouth.

'Is this the lady you were looking for, Daddy?' she asked. 'You'll have to tell the policeman I found her, won't you?'

CHAPTER FOURTEEN

THE hotel stood in Piccadilly. Large and impressive, it was one of the accepted pillars of the establishment, and although Camilla had passed it often enough she had never been inside.

The client must be wealthy if he could take up residence in such a hotel, Camilla thought wryly as the taxi she had hired outside the law office set her down outside the hotel. The wonder was that Mr Bayliss hadn't insisted on dealing with this client personally. Everyone in the office knew he kept the plum assignments for himself.

But on this occasion he had asked Camilla to handle it. Mr Victor, the client, wanted to change his will, and Mr Bayliss had suggested Camilla should deal with it. And, because he was such an important client, she had been asked to go to him, rather than the other way about. Mr Victor apparently kept a suite in the hotel. So much easier, Mr Bayliss had said, than having to bother about the upkeep of a house, or staffing problems.

Camilla hadn't been too keen to accept the assignment. It wasn't normally her brief to draw up testamentary documents. Mr Bayliss usually dealt with all of that. He liked being appointed executor, and handling the financial bequests.

But, for once, Mr Bayliss had insisted he was too busy to leave the office. Besides, he said, the experience would be good for her. Her attitude towards their more affluent clients needed to be refined.

Which meant he thought she was too keen to handle the less lucrative cases they took on, Camilla acknowledged. But the stream of harried men and women, whose lack of forward thinking had landed them with bills to pay and no money to pay them, always aroused her concern. And, because she had compassion, they were invariably shunted into her office. In fact, Camilla had compassion for anyone who found themselves obliged to seek the advice of a solicitor. However, most often it was the fact that they had little money that had brought them there in the first place.

Drawing up this will was something else. It wasn't that Camilla didn't consider it important. She did. It was just that she had other cases, back at the office, that she would have preferred to deal with. Cases that didn't involve going to large hotels.

Not that she had anything against large hotels, she thought ruefully. Large hotels, like large houses and large cars, were simply not important to her. She supposed the godmother who had provided for her in her youth was mostly responsible. Aunt Rebecca, as she had liked to be called, had had everything that money could buy, but she hadn't been content. Camilla's own parents had enjoyed a much more satisfying life. And, although their tragic deaths had left their daughter an orphan, they had left Camilla with the intrinsic belief that happiness couldn't be bought.

Camilla sighed, and pushed through the revolving door into the lobby of the hotel. Who was she kidding? she asked herself impatiently as she crossed the discreetly carpeted foyer to the reception desk. She hadn't thought about her parents' precepts in years. It wasn't their mandate for a good life she was thinking of. It was Virginia's attempted destruction of her own.

'My name's Miss Richards,' she said to the man behind the reception desk. 'I have an appointment with Mr Victor in Suite 904. Will you let him know I'm here?'

She looked around the foyer as the clerk consulted with his superior. Whether she wanted to think about it or not, the last time she had been in a hotel of this size she had been in Honolulu, and the associations it engendered were the real reason she hadn't wanted to come.

'Ah, yes. Miss Richards?'

An older man behind the desk attracted her attention, and Camilla managed a thin smile. 'Yes?'

'Mr Victor has left instructions that you are to go straight up, Miss Richards. The lift is just on your left.

If you take it to the ninth floor Mr Victor's valet will meet you.'

'Thanks.'

Camilla was glad of the activity, but, riding up in the confines of the somewhat less than high-speed lift, she was again forced to confront the memories that plagued her. Memories of riding the metal capsule to Alex's office; memories of Alex making love to her in that huge, sunlit room . . .

No, not *making love* to her, she corrected herself firmly. He hadn't made love to her then; indeed, he had *never* made love to her. Their relationship had been confined to two rather frenzied encounters, neither of which had ended very satisfactorily.

Which was just as well, she conceded steadily. Their alliance had been unwilling at best; at worst, it had been a disaster. There had never been any future in such an association. The circumstances had been unnatural, to say the least, and she had been merely the recipient of Alex's frustration.

That it hadn't been that way for her was just too bad. It wasn't as if she had ever not been aware of the true situation. Alex had never deceived her; he had never made any promises. They had just been two people caught up in an emotional hurricane. And hurricanes had casualties, didn't they? She was simply one of them.

Of course, the eleven weeks and six days since she had left Hawaii should have been sufficient time to provide for her complete recovery. The horror of the night on Alex's yacht, and Grant's subsequent arrest for attempted murder, were not things she wanted to remember—but she couldn't forget. Maybe if, like Virginia and Maria, she had been able to share what had happened with somebody, if she had had the chance to try and rebuild her life on the basis of those past mistakes, she, too, could have learned to live with what had happened. But she was just a bystander, an outsider who had inadvertently become implicated in events that had no bearing on her life. Whatever happened to Alex and Virginia in the future, she would not be involved. Hers had been only a minor role, anyway. The unwary catalyst who had altered everyone's life except her own.

Still, she was glad Virginia had survived Grant's treachery. She would never have forgiven herself if she had been the innocent cause of her friend's death. But then, when she'd flown out to Hawaii she had had no idea that Virginia was playing such a dangerous game. Or that Grant might be desperate enough to try and kill her friend when he discovered she herself had turned against him.

It was easy enough to explain his motives. No one but Virginia knew of his involvement in her disappearance, or of the fact that he had used her addiction to seduce her into doing what he wanted. Even Maria had been kept in ignorance of his identity. It had been a carefully planned scheme to rob Alex of his control of the Conti Corporation.

Oh, Camilla didn't understand all of it. The explanations she had been given—mostly by Alex's father—had hinged on the fact that, after his sister's husband had deserted her, Alex's father had transferred ten per cent of the shares he had inherited in the corporation to Grant's mother, and ten per cent to Grant himself. It appeared that, at present, the majority of the shares in the corporation were divided between Alex, Alex's father, Grant's mother and Grant, with Alex holding the controlling interest. However, if Virginia had been able to persuade Alex to make ten per cent of his shares over to her, as part of a divorce settlement, Grant would ultimately have married Virginia, and with hers and his mother's shares he would have had the power to take over the company.

It had all sounded highly speculative, and Camilla hadn't honestly been able to see Alex allowing such a thing to happen. But then she remembered that Grant had had control of his daughter, and, obviously, if Maria's future was in jeopardy, he might have had no choice.

Which explained, in part, Virginia's growing fears for her and Maria's safety. Grant had been playing for high stakes; and not just for money, as Camilla had at first imagined. He wanted wealth, but he also wanted power, and Virginia's addiction had given him the perfect weapon.

It was only when Camilla had come on the scene that he had had problems. Until then he had believed that Virginia was completely in his thrall, that she would do whatever he wanted so long as she continued to get the drugs she craved. But in her more rational moments Virginia had realised how fragile her position would be once Grant had what he wanted. And she was already beginning to suspect that he was more ruthless than she had ever thought.

Her letter to Camilla hadn't been as unthinking as Camilla had thought when she'd arrived to find Virginia was missing. It hadn't just been a letter: it had been a cry for help; a desperate attempt to deter Grant before it was too late.

Camilla supposed Grant must have begun to have suspicions even then. He must have realised that Virginia had written to her friend while he was setting up his plans for her supposed disappearance. The fact that he had kept the actual date of her departure from Virginia, and Camilla had arrived too late to effect any last-minute hitch, had been fortuitous. But when he had discovered that Virginia had phoned Camilla, and that she was obviously having second thoughts about what they were doing, the situation had deteriorated rapidly.

By the time Virginia had followed Camilla into the Hyatt Regency that day she had been really scared. Grant was getting desperate, partly because Camilla's arrival had complicated matters, and partly because Virginia was proving such an unreliable accomplice. He was beginning to realise that the longer this went on the less likely Virginia was to go through with it, and without her participation his plans would come to nothing.

And, unless he could rely on Virginia's total commitment, his own future was in jeopardy, Alex's father had told Camilla sadly. It had obviously hurt Vittorio to talk of his own family in this way, but Grant's behaviour had destroyed any love he had felt for his nephew. There was no way Grant could abandon the scheme and let Virginia go, he went on ruefully. Knowing what she did about him, she would always be a threat.

Then, when Virginia had told him—for protection, Vittorio thought—that she had actually seen Camilla, and talked to her, Grant had panicked. That night he had returned to the yacht. While she had slept he had administered what he'd believed to be a fatal overdose, imagining, no doubt, that everyone would think Virginia had inadvertently killed herself. It was only when Alex had phoned to give him the news that Virginia and Maria had been found that he'd realised he had made a mistake. Virginia wasn't dead; she was alive . . . if only barely. She had dragged herself to the phone and told Alex where she was before she had collapsed. That was when she had been rushed to the hospital in Honolulu, and the doctors had told Alex she stood a chance of making it.

Camilla shivered now, even in the rococo splendour of the lift. Remembering that morning, and her own subsequent imprisonment on board Alex's yacht, still had the power to chill her blood. Would Grant have killed her? she wondered. It was a question she didn't want to answer. Sufficient to say that when he left her without food or water it was a possibility he must have considered.

Of course, Alex had had no notion that Grant might consider using Camilla as a hostage. At that time his suspicions of Grant had been only that—suspicions. Virginia was saying nothing . . . yet; and Maria was mercifully innocent. But Grant knew it was only a matter of time before the truth came out, and his abduction of Camilla had been a last desperate attempt to avoid being arrested.

He might have got away with it, too, if Maria hadn't left her doll on the yacht. When he had arrived at the hospital no one had questioned the fact that he was alone, and it was not until some hours later that Alex had discovered Camilla was missing. Grant's story then, that she had asked him to drop her in town, could only be accepted. Short of calling him a liar, there was nothing Alex could do, and, with Virginia in Intensive Care, his priorities were obvious.

That he had been worried about Camilla was apparent from his reactions when they'd found her. But then other matters had claimed his attention, not least the police's issuing a warrant for Grant's detention.

That was how Camilla came to hear most of the story from Alex's father. After she'd left the hospital, after undergoing a thorough examination to ensure she suffered no physical ill effects from her night's imprisonment, Alex's parents had insisted she stay with them until her return flight to England could be arranged. They knew nothing of what had taken place between her and their son, of course, but they had never been really happy with her staying in Alex's house.

And Camilla had been eager to comply. Now that her ordeal was over, and Grant had been arrested, Alex was spending every moment at Virginia's bedside. It was obvious that her brief involvement in their lives was over, and she couldn't wait to leave the island and put it all behind her. Indeed, she had tried not to think about that aspect of the affair. To do so was too painful to be borne. All she really wanted was to get back to London, and normality. To forget Alex Conti and the traumatic effect he had had on her life.

So, here she was, she thought now, three months later, and almost entirely her old self again. She interviewed plaintiffs, prepared briefs, went to court to defend her clients against social injustice and sex discrimination—and cried herself to sleep most nights...

The lift slowed, and came to a stop at the ninth floor, and Camilla determinedly put on her official face. After all, this was quite a compliment Mr Bayliss had paid her, giving her this opportunity to deal directly with one of his more important clients. Several eyebrows had been raised in the office when it was revealed where she was going, and those members of the company who considered themselves more senior than Camilla had not been averse to making their feelings felt. If they had only known she would have gladly given them the opportunity to go in her place, Camilla thought resignedly. She preferred the hectic rhythm of the office. Then she didn't have time to think.

The elaborately gilded lift doors opened, and Camilla made a hasty inspection of her appearance. She was wearing a neat black suit, the hem of which was only marginally questionable for a serious meeting, a cream Gatsby shirt with shiny gold buttons, and knee-high leather boots, without heels, that emphasised the shapely calves beneath. As usual, her only misgivings were about her hair. Since her return from Hawaii she had had it cut and styled, and now that the perm had grown out it hung, silky and straight, to her shoulders. Far too conspicuous for a lawyer, she knew, but, short of having the colour changed, there was little she could do.

She stepped out of the lift seconds later to find an elderly black man standing waiting for her. Mr Victor's valet, she presumed. If he was younger than his employer, then her client must be in his late sixties at least.

'Miss Richards?' he asked, but it was only a perfunctory enquiry. He had been advised of her imminent arrival, and as she was the only occupant of the lift it was highly unlikely that she could be anyone else.

'Yes,' she responded now. 'I'm Camilla Richards. How do you do?'

'I do fine, thank you, ma'am,' the man replied, his gnarled face softening with the semblance of a smile. 'Will you come with me? Mr—ah—Victor is waiting for you.'

The corridor was wide, and high, and carpeted in an eggshell shade of blue. There were little stars of silver-grey broadloom set into the edges of the carpet, and Camilla found herself concentrating on these as she accompanied the valet to Mr Victor's suite. She was also rehearsing how she should begin the interview. If Mr Victor was old he might expect her to advise him about trusts and other tax-free privileges. She was glad she had made some notes and brought them with her. They were presently residing in the briefcase at her side.

Suite 904 had double doors and the valet opened both of them. Much as a magician might throw open the doors of a magic cabinet to reveal his latest trick, the man threw open the doors to the suite, and invited Camilla inside. 'Miss Richards, *signore*,' he said with a strangely undeferential smile, and the briefcase dropped from Camilla's nerveless fingers as Alex Conti turned from gazing out of the windows.

'Thanks, Carlo,' he said as Camilla hastily picked up her briefcase again. 'You can leave us now. Miss—er— Richards and I have some things to talk about.'

'Yes, *signore*.'

Carlo bowed and, stepping outside again, closed the doors with almost as much of a flourish as he had opened them. But the difference was that this time Camilla knew exactly who she was dealing with, and her heart hammered so loudly that she was sure Alex must hear it.

And, because she was so shocked—and confused—Camilla found she couldn't say anything. Not 'Hello' or 'How are you?' or even 'What are you doing here?' Instead, she looked rather stupidly around the apartment, admiring its luxurious appointments without really seeing them. Anything rather than look at Alex, who seemed perfectly willing to allow her time to recover.

He should have warned her, she thought unsteadily, her gaze flickering over damask-covered walls and striped Regency chairs. She supposed it had amused him to invite her here under false pretences, but that still didn't explain why he had done it. Whose idea had it been? His—or Virginia's?

She swallowed convulsively. Yes, of course. It was exactly the sort of thing Virginia would have thought of. Her way of defusing a rather embarrassing situation. Though why she had felt the need to come here and explain herself to her, Camilla couldn't imagine...

'I hope you didn't mind the subterfuge,' Alex said quietly, and, realising she couldn't go on avoiding looking at him, Camilla forced herself to do so. After all, if this was Virginia's idea of a joke, her pride couldn't be allowed to ruin the effect.

Even so, it wasn't easy to meet his dark-eyed gaze, and after only a few seconds her eyes darted away. But she found it wasn't that easy to ignore his lean-limbed body, and almost against her will she noticed how tense he was. It was there in the stiff way he was holding himself, in the unnaturally taut bunching of his fists. And, although the pale grey shirt he was wearing accentuated the natural darkness of his skin, his face was strangely paler, his features rigid and thin.

Of course, it had been an arduous time for him, Camilla reminded herself impatiently. Apart from his anxieties over Maria—and his wife—there had been Grant's betrayal to deal with, and his subsequent arrest.

It couldn't have been easy for any of them, and Alex's role had naturally been the most difficult.

'Why... Victor?' she asked now, as much to give herself time to formulate a response as anything, and Alex's lips tightened.

'My second name is Vittorio—like my father's,' he explained, equally objectively, and Camilla forced a smile to lighten her expression.

'Who... whose idea was this?' she asked, realising these were pointless questions, but unable to broach what was obviously in the forefront of both their minds, and Alex frowned.

'Whose?' he echoed a little blankly. 'Why—mine, of course. I... don't understand the question. Who else's could it be?'

Camilla shrugged, holding the briefcase in front of her with both hands, feeling more and more bewildered as the minutes passed. 'I thought perhaps... Virginia,' she ventured, saying the other woman's name with a feeling of relief. There, it was out, she thought triumphantly. And, if it had been painful, at least it hadn't killed her.

'*Virginia!*' said Alex now, and his voice was so harsh and strange that Camilla stumbled into explanations.

'Well, yes,' she said, speaking quickly. 'I thought perhaps she and Maria were with you. I know Virginia used to love shopping in London, and if Maria hasn't been before there are so many things to see——'

'*For God's sake!*' Alex's oath would have been enough to silence her, she thought, but when it was uttered as he crossed the space between them it was doubly daunting. 'Are you crazy?' he demanded, halting in front of her, and gazing down at her with savage eyes. 'Why would I bring *Virginia* to London with me? You know how I feel about Virginia. My God, what do you think I am? Some kind of saint?'

Camilla forced herself to breathe, and the air gushed out of her lungs in jerky little gasps. 'I—just thought——'

'Yes?' He was so close that she could see every pore of his skin, every crease around his eyes and mouth, every tiny variation in pigment where the sun had scored the flesh. 'What did you think, I wonder? That if you walked out on me I'd turn to Virginia for consolation?'

Camilla swallowed again. It was becoming a distinct necessity to do so, and she could feel the muscles in her throat working overtime to cope with the output of her glands. 'I—didn't—walk—out—on—you,' she enunciated carefully, and then uttered a little shriek when he clamped his hands to her shoulders.

'What did you do, then?' he grated. 'Oh, I appreciate why you didn't want to press charges against Grant, and my father explained how you wanted to put what had happened on the yacht behind you. That I can understand. But…leaving the island! Taking the first available flight back to London! That I *can't* understand. You must have known I'd want to see you again. Or did that side of our relationship mean nothing to you?'

Camilla moistened her lips. His hands were hurting her, but she was hardly aware of it. The briefcase she was holding at the length of her arms was bumping against her knees and his, but she was hardly aware of that either. Her gaze was focused on his mouth, on the thin upper lip and the full lower one, and the glimpse of milk-white teeth she could see between.

'I…*our* relationship?' she got out unevenly, and Alex swore, rather colourfully.

'Yes, our relationship,' he agreed, his voice thickening as his gaze dropped to the nervous circling of her tongue. 'We did have a relationship, didn't we? Or was it all my imagination?'

'But . . . Virginia——'

'Is no longer my wife,' said Alex unsteadily, and Camilla's eyes widened.

'She's . . . all right——'

'As she'll ever be.' But Alex could see Camilla's doubts, and, controlling his impatience, he went on. 'She's nearing the end of yet another rehabilitation programme, as it happens. And no charges are being brought against her, if that's what's worrying you. Now, does that clarify the situation? Or would you like me to draw you a picture?'

Camilla quivered, and then, as if it was important to maintain some kind of normality here, she said, 'Could...could I put my briefcase down?'

'*God!*'

With a gesture of frustration, Alex released her then, and, as Camilla set her briefcase on the velvet carpet at her feet, he walked back to the windows. He was in his shirt-sleeves, and although it was not a very cheerful day outside the light from the windows silhouetted his hunched shoulders beneath the fine silk. He had his back to her now as if the last few minutes had never happened, and Camilla shifted her weight from one foot to the other, not quite knowing how to proceed.

Buttoning and unbuttoning the jacket of her suit, she sought about for some suitable opening, and found it in asking about his daughter. 'How...how is Maria?' she asked, unable to absorb anything of what he had told her. 'I wanted to thank her for forgetting her doll. If she hadn't——'

'You might not have made it. I know,' said Alex flatly, but without turning to look at her again. 'Believe me, she knows how important her contribution was. She's been told often enough.'

'By you?' ventured Camilla, barely audibly, but he heard her.

'By me, by her mother, by her grandparents,' he agreed almost detachedly. 'My aunt, Grant's mother, is particularly grateful. Attempted murder is a serious charge, but an actual death would have been something else.'

Camilla dipped her head. 'And...otherwise Maria's all right?' It was all she could say. 'No...ill effects from her confinement or anything?'

'Not specially.' Alex paused to run a hand round the back of his neck. 'She does tend to worry if I go away. But Mama Lu's a tower of strength, and her grandparents make sure she's never lonely.'

Camilla glanced about her. 'So where is she? Is she with you?'

'No.'

Alex's response was bleak, and Camilla pressed her hands together. 'No?'

'No,' he said again, continuing to gaze out of the window, supporting himself with his hands that were now spread wide on the sill. 'No, this was one trip I needed to make alone. Lately I've found some things are more important than Maria's feelings. Isn't that strange? Six months ago she was the most important person in my life.'

Camilla took an involuntary step towards him. She knew what he was saying, and subconsciously she was doing what her heart was telling her to do. But still it was difficult to believe what she was hearing, and, although her feet were moving, her brain was holding her back.

Nevertheless, she was closing the space between them, and presently, if she stretched out her hand, she could touch his back. Such a rigid back, she thought, putting out her hand, and then withdrawing it again. Oh, God, she wanted to believe him. But she was afraid of being hurt even more.

When he turned, her instinctive reaction was to back away from him again, but she forced herself to stand her ground. And she realised, as she looked over his shoulder, that he had watched her halting progress reflected in the window. He didn't touch her, however. He merely propped his hips on the sill, and waited for her to speak.

'I—er—I'm glad you came,' she said lamely, her gaze shifting to the area of grey silk covering his pectoral muscles. A muscle was jerking beneath the fabric as if his body, like hers, refused to obey the dictates of his brain, and she was distracted. She wanted to reach out and soothe his nervous flesh; she wanted to touch him. But her hands flexed helplessly, not knowing how to begin.

'Are you?' Alex asked at last, and she guessed he was not about to humiliate himself again. He was here; he had told her why. Why couldn't she believe it?

'I didn't walk out on you,' she said, repeating the words she had used earlier, and one of his dark eyebrows arched. 'I didn't,' she went on. 'But I couldn't stay with your parents indefinitely. And ... and I didn't know how you felt, did I?'

Alex bent his head. 'Didn't you?'

'No.' Camilla took a steadying breath. 'You were never around——'

His head came up then. 'You know why!'

'Y...es.' She could feel the beads of perspiration standing on her forehead, but she continued to meet his gaze. 'But I thought...I mean...there was Virginia...'

Alex's eyes narrowed. 'Did you want me to take Virginia back?' he asked savagely, and Camilla knew she couldn't go on playing this game of cat and mouse.

'No,' she said, shaking her head violently. 'No, of course not. But—but——'

'What did you want, then?' persisted Alex, determined to have her say it, and Camilla's shoulders sagged.

'You,' she breathed, scarcely above a whisper. 'Only you,' and, with a muffled oath, Alex jerked her towards him.

He was still sitting on the window-sill, and when he pulled her between his legs the powerful muscles of his thighs imprisoned her. But she was taller than he was in that position, and, although his hands came up to grip the sides of her head, it wasn't enough.

With a lithe movement he pushed himself up, and the urgent pressure of his mouth sought hers. His groan of satisfaction filled her senses and she leaned into him eagerly as he raked her mouth with his tongue.

He slid the jacket of her suit off her shoulders, while his lips played havoc with her emotions. Then, drawing her quivering arms around him, he lowered his head to her neck, brushing the fiery hair aside, and creating a fire of his own every place he kissed her. His tongue was damp against her flesh, laving her skin with dew, yet searing every nerve in her body. For a few moments it was impossible to speak, only to feel, and when Camilla finally found the strength to say anything it was a murmured appeal that he should never stop.

'Don't worry, I won't,' Alex muttered roughly, and his seductive mouth sought hers again.

He had drawn her hands behind him and left them there, but now Camilla's palms spread against his back. His shirt was in the way, and she tugged it free of the waistband of his trousers so that she could touch his skin. His spine arched beneath her tentative exploration, and she trailed her fingers down below his belt, seeking the hollow cavity at its base. The unknowing sexuality of her touch drove his pelvis towards her, and the bones of his hips grazed her softer frame.

'God, I want you,' he said in a strangled voice, and Camilla's limbs melted at that husky admission. It was what she wanted, too, urgently, achingly, and the moisture she could feel between her legs was proof of her eager response.

She could feel him against her, hard and masculine, and when he dipped his head so that his tongue could stroke the swollen tips of her breasts she felt her knees turn to water. She had never realised her body contained such an abundance of feeling, and her desire to show him how much she cared became an actual physical need inside her.

Her fingers fumbled with the buttons of his shirt, the urgency to feel his body against hers overwhelming all her inhibitions. She didn't care any more if this was for real or just a fleeting temptation so far as he was concerned. She wanted him. She wanted to feel him a part of her. And, if that was all he wanted of her, for now it was enough.

'Take it easy,' he groaned when her hands were drawn downwards to brush the taut pressure beneath his zip. 'I've waited so long for this moment, and I'm not sure how much more I can take.'

As he spoke he peeled the Gatsby shirt off her shoulders, some of the gold buttons scattering across the floor. Then, as his mouth deposited a bracelet of kisses across the creamy skin of her throat, he released the single clip of her bra, and the rosy fullness of her breasts surged into his hands.

'God, you're beautiful!' he breathed, holding the pale globes in his palms, and burying his face in the hollow between. Then he took each dusky nipple into his mouth in turn, nipping them gently with his teeth, before sucking softly at each proud apex.

When her fingers went to his belt, however, he cupped her buttocks and lifted her so that her legs went automatically around him. It brought that sexually aroused part of him so much closer to her own throbbing core, and she wrapped her arms around his neck and brought his mouth back to hers. This time it was her tongue that was the invader, and with a moan of anguish Alex stumbled blindly into the adjoining bedroom.

The bed was big and wide, which was just as well, because Alex was incapable of making any rational survey of his surroundings. He knew the general whereabouts of the bed, and when his knees hit the side they both tumbled on to the mattress. Camilla was on her back, with Alex on top of her, and, although there was nothing particularly elegant about their position, it was very satisfying to both of them.

Even so, Camilla was still wearing her skirt and boots, and Alex's trousers were only partially unfastened. It took a few hectic seconds to remedy this state of affairs, and then their positions were resumed, albeit with a certain amount of heavy breathing from Alex.

'Please—now...' Camilla whimpered, winding her arms around his neck, and although he made a sound of protest he couldn't deny what his tormented body was telling him. With a sigh of anguish he parted her legs and pushed his pulsating shaft into her moist honeycomb, and she let out a little cry as the pure size of him spread her unwary muscles.

'Oh,' she breathed, taking short gulping breaths as he began to move inside her. The swelling ripples of delight, that previously she had only touched upon, were already overtaking and overwhelming her, and, although she was sure a woman was not supposed to be aroused so quickly, she couldn't help herself. Alex's nude body was crushing hers, the exquisite heat of him, filling and expanding her to an unimaginable extent, was driving her to a mindless state of ecstasy. And all coherent thought splintered when the wet force of his release spurted into her...

CHAPTER FIFTEEN

'I'M SORRY.'

Camilla was drifting on a limitless sea of pleasure when Alex's words brought her back to an awareness of where she was, and what she was doing, and her eyes darkened bewilderedly.

'You are?' She didn't understand his words, and as usual she jumped to the wrong conclusion. 'Well, don't be. I was as much to blame——'

'To blame?' Now it was Alex's turn to look confused, and he propped himself up, with his elbows at either side of her head. 'What are you talking about?'

She was intensely aware that he was still a part of her. Their bodies were still joined, and, even as she looked up at him through emotionally dazed eyes, she could feel him hardening again inside her.

'Well,' she said, moistening her lips. 'I thought——'

'Yes?' He bent his head to brush his tongue against her temple and she quivered. 'What did you think?' he asked, his movement causing the slight covering of hair on his chest to tickle the sensitive tips of her breasts. 'You're not going to tell me this was a mistake, are you?'

'I—well...'

Alex's eyes narrowed. 'Are you?' he repeated warily, and she quickly shook her head.

'Of course not.'

'Then what?'

'Oh...' She sighed. 'It was you. You said you were sorry——'

'For losing control,' he told her huskily. 'God, Camilla, it wasn't meant to be this way. I intended to love you by degrees, not throw you on the bed and practically take you by force!'

'You didn't take me by force!' she exclaimed, her lips parting now. 'I wanted you just as much as...as you wanted me. You must know that.'

'Even so——'

'It was...fantastic,' she breathed, putting up her hands and sliding them into the silky dampness of his hair. 'For me, anyway.'

Alex's mouth twisted. 'I trust you don't expect an answer to that,' he told her wryly. 'Right now I'm not in a mood to trade unnecessary remarks of that nature. Suffice it to say, you've gone a small way to solving a problem I've had for the past three months.'

Camilla's lips parted. 'A problem?' she echoed swiftly. 'What kind of problem?'

'Wanting you,' retorted Alex with some heat. 'Don't pretend I've made any secret of the fact. God knows, you must be the last to know. My family have been left in no doubt about my feelings for the past several weeks. Loving you has made me hell to live with, believe me.'

Loving you!

Camilla trembled. She found the notion that Alex might have been as miserable since she'd left Hawaii as she had been herself very appealing, and the little smile that tugged at the corner of her mouth revealed the fact.

'I suppose you find that amusing,' he muttered, and the amazing realisation that he was as unsure of himself now as she had been earlier made her hasten to reassure him.

'Not...amusing,' she denied huskily, taking his face between her hands and drawing his mouth down to hers. 'Incredible, perhaps,' she added against his lips, and Alex found himself incapable of continuing this conversation.

His mouth was gentle as he kissed her, once, twice, turning his head from side to side, so that she was left weak and breathless. Then, feeling her instinctive response, his mouth hardened, and the pressure of his tongue drove all other thoughts aside. She knew him now; knew the hot possession of him inside her; knew the feel, and the taste, and the clean musky smell of his maleness. He was hers, she thought dizzily, just as she was his, and the liquid heat he created was like a fire in her veins.

This time their lovemaking was slower, more deliberate, Alex using his undoubted skill to bring Camilla to the brink of sensation time and time again, until her senses were screaming for a fulfilment he was intentionally withholding. He used his power over her body to arouse her to a complete awareness of her own sexual potential, and when she tumbled into the heady chasm he had created for her she was mindless, exhausted, and totally content . . .

Some time later Alex rolled on to his side, taking her with him, and Camilla buried her face against his chest as she said softly, 'I love you, I love you, I love you.'

'Do you?' Alex took her chin in his hand, and tipped her flushed face up to his. 'Do you mean that?'

'Do I have to prove it again?' she asked ruefully, the colour that was never far from the surface of her skin deepening the brilliance of her green eyes. 'You must know I do. I just didn't . . . believe . . .'

'That I loved you too?' Alex finished for her softly, and she nodded. 'Oh, sweetheart, I think I fell in love with you that first day, when I saw you at the airport. Only there was nothing I could do about it then. But when I found you waiting at the house—well, nothing was quite the same after that.'

'Wasn't it?' Camilla found she liked this kind of exchange after all. Propping herself up on one elbow, she looked down at him adoringly, hardly able to believe even now that this was actually happening. She stroked the outline of his lips with one exploring finger. 'I thought you resented my being there.'

'I did.' Alex pulled her teasing fingers into his mouth and bit them hard. He sighed. 'You have to understand my feelings at that time. My opinion of women was at an all-time low, and the last thing I thought I needed was some smart-ass lady lawyer telling me what I should and shouldn't do.'

'I didn't do that!'

Camilla was indignant, and Alex grinned at her struggles to extract her smarting fingers from his hold. 'You did,' he argued, caressing the tiny scars he had made

and soothing them with his tongue. 'And, I guess, subconsciously I was aware of the dangers you represented.'

'Dangers?'

'To my peace of mind,' explained Alex huskily. 'Dear
God, after my experiences with Virginia I had no intention
of ever getting involved with anyone else. I'd already
decided that if I got Maria back safely I'd take steps to
ensure that nothing like that ever happened again. I was
going to get a divorce, whatever threats Virginia cared
to throw my way, and marrying someone else was simply
not on the cards.'

Camilla's tongue appeared. 'Marrying someone else?'
she echoed. 'Does that mean what . . . what I think it
means?'

Alex gave her an old-fashioned look. 'Stop fishing.'

'No.' Camilla caught her lower lip between her teeth.
'I'm not. It's just that . . .'

Alex regarded her quizzically. 'You're not going to
turn me down, are you?'

'Oh—no.' Camilla shook her head helplessly.
'Not . . . not if it's what you want.'

'Believe me, it's what I want,' said Alex heavily. 'God,
I don't think I could stand another few weeks like those
I've just spent. You've no idea how hard it's been.'

'Oh—I think I have,' murmured Camilla huskily,
bending her head to brush his temple with her lips. 'It's
just . . . unbelievable, that's all.'

'Why?'

'Well—it has been almost three months——'

'D'you think I don't know that?' Alex's eyes softened,
and he ran his long fingers up into her hair. 'Believe me,
I have the scars to prove it. But, baby, England is the
other side of the world, and, like it or not, I had to stay
in Honolulu until that business with Grant was tied up.'

'Is . . . is he . . . ?'

'In prison?' Alex shook his head. 'No. No, he's not.
My father found him a good lawyer, and after some
negotiation Virginia decided not to press charges. I guess
she decided she didn't need any more adverse publicity,
and, although it wasn't easy, the family name remains
more or less intact.'

'I see.'

But Camilla still looked troubled, and Alex pulled her down to him and cradled her head against his shoulder. 'Believe me,' he said, 'I wanted to nail that bastard just as much as you did, but my aunt means a lot to me—to all of us—and she was the one who would suffer most. So...Grant's got what you might call a "stay of execution", with the sure and certain knowledge that if he transgresses again he doesn't get a second chance.'

'You mean he's still working for you?'

Camilla was horrified, and Alex chuckled. 'Oh, no,' he said softly. 'I'm not that benevolent. Grant's sacrificed any chance he ever had of running the Conti Corporation. Forfeiting the shares he had in the company was only one of the demands his lawyer agreed to. Leaving Hawaii was another. At present he's in Venezuela, working for a subsidiary of Conti Oil, with a good friend of my father's to keep an eye on him. I don't think he'll trouble us again. Grant has too fine a liking for his own skin.'

'Ah!' Camilla breathed more easily. But there was still one more thing she had to ask. 'And...and what about Virginia?'

'What about Virginia?' Alex frowned. 'I've told you about her. She's in a clinic——'

'Yes. Yes, I know that.' Camilla sighed. 'I just meant——'

'Does she know about us?' prompted Alex gently, and she nodded again. 'Well,' he went on, 'the answer is yes. I told her. Right about the time she told me she thought we'd be good for one another.'

'No!' Camilla lifted her head.

'Yes.' Alex was complacent. 'Virginia may be many things, but she's no fool. She knew how I felt when you went back to England. God, I wasn't fit to live with. I knew I couldn't go tearing after you, not with Virginia in the hospital, Grant in custody, and Maria still unwilling to let me out of her sight. I guess she thought she was doing me a favour by telling me that she thought you felt the same. The trouble was I couldn't prove it, and the last few weeks have been a living hell!'

Camilla snuggled down again, sliding her leg between his, and exulting in the unfamiliar intimacy. 'So...you got a divorce?' she ventured, and he groaned.

'That was my mother's idea. You have to remember family is important to my parents. My mother may not be of Italian extraction, but she's been married to my father for more than forty years, and I guess she's absorbed his customs by osmosis. Anyway, her contribution was that maybe you left because I was married. She said she thought you were a decent girl, and that you'd never consider having a relationship with a married man.'

Camilla chuckled now. 'Oh, dear. If she only knew!'

'Yes, well—let's keep it our secret, shall we?' suggested Alex laughingly. 'So long as she can attend our wedding I'm sure she won't make too many objections.'

'Our wedding!'

Camilla's voice was dreamy, and Alex couldn't resist bestowing a lingering kiss on her parted lips. 'Our wedding,' he agreed huskily, easing himself closer. 'And it had better be soon, because I don't intend to go back without you.'

Camilla returned his kiss, and then, with her fingertips caressing his cheek, she said, 'Will...will Maria mind, do you think?'

'Maria?' Alex brought her fingers to his lips again. 'I don't think you have to worry about Maria.'

'But she is going to live with us, isn't she?' exclaimed Camilla anxiously. 'I mean...Virginia...'

'Virginia never wanted Maria,' Alex told her softly. 'Our marriage was a mistake, from start to finish. Maria was just the innocent result, that's all. You must know if she hadn't been around I wouldn't have tried so hard to sustain the pretence. And it was a pretence, believe me. Only I had the money Virginia needed to support her habit, and I—well, I was foolish enough to think that it was better for Maria to have two parents, instead of only one.'

'But...do you think she'll like me?'

'Well, she already feels she has a certain...obligation to make sure nothing else bad happens to you,' remarked Alex drily. 'I mean, I've already told you that she understands how important her contribution to your discovery was. Well, let me tell you, that's not an obligation Maria takes lightly.'

Camilla smiled. 'Really?'

'You'd better believe it,' Alex advised her wryly, and Camilla thought how delightful a prospect that was.

A year later Alex took Camilla out to dinner. It was their first outing together since the birth of their baby son, and Alex had been desperate to get his wife alone.

'You know,' he said, putting his hands across the table and imprisoning hers between them, 'I never used to think I was the jealous type. But lately I've had to revise my opinion.'

Camilla's eyes danced. 'Jealous?' she exclaimed. 'What have you got to be jealous about?'

'Not what—*who*!' amended Alex ruefully. 'Our son, of course. James Alexander Victor, to be precise. For the past three months it's been impossible for us to be alone together.'

Camilla smiled. 'Well,' she said consideringly, 'we do sleep together, darling...'

Alex's eyes darkened. 'When we're allowed to.'

'Oh, Alex!' Camilla chuckled. 'You wouldn't have wanted me to let him starve, would you?'

'No.' Alex conceded that point. 'But I'm glad he's going to be bottle-fed from now on.' He raised her hands to his lips. 'I like having you all to myself, and our having a baby straight away wasn't exactly in my scheme of things.'

'Then you shouldn't have pretended you wanted your will changing when you had something else in mind,' Camilla reminded him laughingly, and Alex had to smile at her undeniable logic.

'All right, all right,' he said. 'So I admit I couldn't keep my hands off you. But let's not have another baby for a while, hmm? Like maybe...ten years?'

Camilla shook her head. 'Well—maybe not quite that long,' she amended, remembering the sensuous pleasure of feeling Alex's baby growing inside her. 'But a couple of years—yes. I could handle that.'

'And me?' enquired Alex softly, and now she brought his hands to her lips.

'Oh, yes,' she said. 'I think I know how to handle you. I'm getting lots of experience.'

'Camilla!'

His husky use of her name reminded her of where they were—in one of the most exclusive hotels in Honolulu—and that bringing that particular light to Alex's eyes was not entirely wise.

'Besides,' she said then, in an effort to divert him, 'I don't think Maria would like it if we produced another baby too soon. James is a doll, and she thinks the world of him, but we'll let her get used to the idea of having a baby brother before we consider giving her a baby sister, too, hmm?'

'Anything you say,' agreed Alex, his eyes dark and slumbrous as they lingered on the dusky hollow between her breasts. Then, glancing round for the waiter, he lifted his hand. 'But right now I think we ought to get some practice. I mean,' his husky teasing tone bringing the colour to her cheeks again, 'they say practice makes perfect, don't they?' And Camilla couldn't argue with that.

Take 4 bestselling love stories FREE

Plus get a FREE surprise gift!

HARLEQUIN
HISTORICAL

CHRISTMAS
·STORIES·1992·

Capture the magic and romance of Christmas in the 1800s
with HARLEQUIN HISTORICAL CHRISTMAS STORIES
1992, a collection of three stories by celebrated historical
authors. The perfect Christmas gift!

Don't miss these heartwarming stories, available in
November wherever Harlequin books are sold:

MISS MONTRACHET REQUESTS by Maura Seger
CHRISTMAS BOUNTY by Erin Yorke
A PROMISE KEPT by Bronwyn Williams

Plus, as an added bonus, you can receive a FREE keepsake
Christmas ornament. Just collect four proofs of purchase
from any November or December 1992 Harlequin or
Silhouette series novels, or from any Harlequin or
Silhouette Christmas collection, and receive a beautiful
dated brass Christmas candle ornament.

Mail this certificate along with four (4) proof-of-purchase coupons plus $1.50 postage and
handling (check or money order—do not send cash), payable to Harlequin Books, to: **In the
U.S.:** P.O. Box 9057, Buffalo, NY 14269-9057; **In Canada:** P.O. Box 622, Fort Erie, Ontario,
L2A 5X3.

**ONE PROOF OF
PURCHASE**

Name: _____
_____
Address: _____
_____
City: _____
State/Province: _____
Zip/Postal Code: _____

HX92POP   093 KAG